DANGEROUSLY CLOSE

Other titles by
SANDRA GLOVER

DANGEROUSLY CLOSE

SANDRA GLOVER

ANDERSEN PRESS LONDON

First published in 2008 by
Andersen Press Limited,
20 Vauxhall Bridge Road, London SW1V 2SA
www.andersenpress.co.uk
www.sandraglover.co.uk

British Library Cataloguing in Publication Data available

ISBN 978 184 270 679 4

Mixed Sources
Product group from well-managed
forests and other controlled sources
www.fsc.org Cert no. TT-COC-0002227
© 1996 Forest Stewardship Council

Typeset by FiSH Books, Enfield, Middx
Printed in the UK by CPI Bookmarque, Croydon, CR0 4TD

1

'I don't want to go,' Scott mumbled.

'Well, don't,' said Kieran. 'Go home, give us all a break. Just don't keep whingeing on about it, OK?'

'Leave it, Kieran,' Dee snapped. 'You're not helping.'

Scott's anxiety had been building from the minute they'd left their grandparents' house, intensifying as they got nearer the school. Now, with the main building clearly visible, Scott had turned so pale Dee was sure he was going to throw up.

'Hey, get a grip, Scott,' she said, gently but firmly. 'It'll be OK. Honest. I'll look out for you at break and lunchtime.'

'Awww, diddums,' said Kieran. 'He's eleven, Dee, not five! An' it's you that's not helping. You'll have him snivelling in a minute.'

Right on cue, Scott started to cry. Not quiet, discreet tears but huge, violent sobs that drew the attention of other kids as they headed onto the drive.

'Shut it,' said Kieran, gripping the back of his brother's neck. 'Do you want to make yourself a target or what? You may as well have "victim" tattooed on your head, the way you're going on.'

Target. Victim. The words hit Dee like physical blows, almost forcing tears to her own eyes. How could Kieran be so stupid, so insensitive? But his words seemed to work. Either that or the death grip, which Kieran was now slowly releasing, had taken effect. Amazingly, Kieran's roughness didn't seem to bother Scott at all. If anyone else had grabbed Scott like that . . .

'He can come with me,' Kieran was saying. 'But just for today, right?'

Dee forced a smile. She wasn't feeling a whole lot better than Scott. The school had seemed fine when they'd been to look round with Gran and Granddad back in June. More than fine. It was smaller than her old school in Liverpool, surrounded by fields rather than houses and noisy traffic. It had a good academic record, priding itself on its friendly, personal touch, or so the headmaster had said. But then, he would, wouldn't he? Right now, with everyone pushing, hyped-up for the first day of term, it didn't seem remotely friendly. It seemed tense, alien, threatening. No wonder Scott was panicking.

Kieran, on the other hand, didn't seem bothered at all. Watching him as he nudged Scott towards the playground, it was hard to believe they were brothers. Kieran was well-built; tall for his age, with his hair closely cropped and a way of looking at people out of fiercely blue eyes that announced he wasn't to be messed with. Whereas Scott...Scott was more like her and Dad. Nothing much to notice about them at all. Average height, mousy-blond hair, greyish-blue eyes. Naturally easy-going. The sort of people who usually just blended in, went with the flow, or at least that's how they used to be.

Dee waited until the boys disappeared round the corner, then she turned into one of the newer buildings on the right. Somewhere in here was the sixth form common room but the narrow beige corridors all looked bewildering similar and she couldn't quite remember which one she was supposed to follow. She was about to pick on someone to ask when she felt a tap on her shoulder. Turning, she saw a girl with short, reddish-brown hair and very tired brown eyes.

'Dee!' the girl gushed, as though they were old friends, rather than people who'd met only once, over two months ago, when the girl had been assigned as Dee's mentor, to help her settle in.

'Oh hi, Hazel,' said Dee, relieved to see someone she knew and hoping that Scott's mentor had been equally keen.

'Come on, this way,' Hazel said, yawning. 'Sorry! We

only got back from our hols at four this morning, would you believe? We were supposed to get back two days ago but with the strike and everything, we've been camping out at the flaming airport, haven't we? Dad was frantic 'cos his mate, who's been looking after our farm, was due on his own holiday today, so Dad was like on the phone every five minutes. It was mad, totally mad. First holiday Dad's had in ten years and he says he's never, ever going again. Anyway, how's youse? Got your house sorted yet?'

'Er, no,' said Dee, surprised by the sudden questions at the end of Hazel's rant. 'We're still with my grandparents, until Dad finds a job.'

'I thought he had one lined up,' said Hazel.

'Yeah but it, er, fell through,' said Dee, wishing she hadn't mentioned her dad.

Mercifully, Hazel didn't follow up with more questions. Instead she pushed open the door to the common room, which seemed a whole lot cleaner and neater than the last time Dee had seen it. It smelled of fresh paint, pine disinfectant and coffee.

'Hey!' said Hazel, heading for the coffee. 'New carpet. Luxury! They've even cleaned the green slime out of the sink, look.'

'Yeah,' said a lad, wearing a deputy head boy badge. 'But they're threatening to close the common room for good if it gets in that state again.'

'Well, you can't blame us, Sanjay!' said Hazel. 'We weren't even in the sixth last year. It's you disgusting lot who had to have the place fumigated.'

'Wasn't us neither, guv,' said Sanjay, putting on a daft voice. 'It was last year's Upper Sixth, wasn't it? At least, that's our story.'

'Anyway,' Hazel said, handing Sanjay his coffee and looking around, 'where's Abbie?'

Sanjay's smile faded.

'I don't know and I don't care,' he said, taking his drink and walking over to some friends on the far side of the room.

'Whoops,' said Hazel, picking up the two remaining plastic cups before heading towards a small table in the corner. 'They must have had another bust up. I've been away for over three weeks, I'm completely out of touch.'

'I think I remember Abbie,' said Dee, sitting down. 'She's your best mate, right? The one with the . . .'

'Loud mouth?'

'Hair, I was going to say!'

'Yeah, that's our Abbie. Wild hair, wild girl. Her and Sanjay have been sort of together for about two years but she dumps him, on average, once a week. What about you? Have you got a bloke?'

'No,' said Dee. 'There was someone, back home but it wasn't serious or anything. It's not like we're going to keep in touch.'

She wasn't going to keep in touch with anyone from back home. She couldn't bear their curiosity, their pity. All that was over, gone, finished. This was a new start, for all of them. A place where no one knew what had happened and, with any luck, would never find out.

'Oh,' said Hazel. 'Well, not to worry. I'm free and single too but who knows? Don't suppose you've got any fit brothers or anything, have you?'

'Two,' said Dee. 'But I think they'd be a bit young for you!'

'Oh that's right!' said Hazel. 'I saw them, when you came to look round. Year 7 and 10, yeah?'

Dee nodded, gulping the rest of her drink as the bell went.

'No need to choke yourself,' said Hazel, getting up slowly. 'Form room's just along the corridor and we've got Mr Jenson. Games teacher,' she added, as though that was supposed to explain something. 'Hey, I wonder where Abbie is, though.'

In the classroom, Hazel led Dee to a table near the back, where a lad was sitting alone. He had light ginger hair, trendy specs and something above his top lip that might, over the next million years or so, evolve into a moustache.

'Dee, this is Joe,' said Hazel. 'My other best mate. He's cool, a sort of honorary girl.'

'Thanks!' said Joe. 'You make out like I'm gay or summat.'

'Nothing wrong with being gay,' said Hazel.

''Cept I'm not,' Joe grumbled.

'I know! All I meant was, you're the sort of guy who keeps his brain cells in his head, instead of his bollocks. It's supposed to be a compliment!'

'Oh, right,' said Joe, as the girls sat down.

They'd done the register and launched into the apparently impossible task of sorting their timetables, when the classroom door burst open and Abbie appeared.

'Sorry,' she said to Mr Jenson, as she breezed past. 'Not a good start, is it? Couldn't seem to get myself sorted.'

'Understandable, Abbie,' said Mr Jenson. 'I mean, you've only had six weeks.'

Dee watched Abbie smile at, but otherwise ignore, Mr Jenson before heading across the classroom towards them. As far as Dee could tell, Abbie had managed to sort herself pretty well. She looked stunning, not to mention about three years older than the rest of them, with her slightly heavy but immaculate make-up, fitted shirt clinging to her incredible figure and, of course, the hair. Masses of dark hair falling in the sort of chaos which must take hours to achieve, glinting with purple highlights that might have looked outrageous on anyone

7

else. All the boys stared as she sashayed past. All except Joe whose eyes remained fixed on Hazel.

'Hazel!' Abbie said, giving her friend a hug, before sitting down. 'I've missed you! I've got so much to tell you. You won't believe what's been happening.'

'Go on, amaze me,' said Hazel, sliding Abbie's timetable towards her.

'I'm in love!' said Abbie, her green eyes positively sparkling as she spoke.

'Wow,' said Hazel. 'I thought from what Sanjay said, you'd split.'

'Not him, you eejit!' said Abbie. 'I wouldn't be in love with Sanjay, would I? I mean, Sanjay's OK but this is different. This is like, totally amazing!'

'Timetables, ladies,' said Mr Jenson as Abbie's voice rose to almost a shriek.

'So who, I mean when, what do you mean?' whispered Hazel.

'He came into the café, the Saturday you went on holiday,' Abbie whispered back, looking alternately at Hazel and Joe, making Dee feel like an eavesdropper, an intruder. 'He kept looking at me, even though I was serving another table, right?'

'Like guys do,' said Hazel.

'Yeah well,' said Abbie. 'But I was so uncool! I just kept smiling at him. Couldn't help it!'

'And?' said Hazel.

'He came over, asked me out.'

'Yeah, I sort of gathered that. I mean what's his name, what's he like?'

'Tom,' said Abbie, drawing the name out, caressing it. 'And he's utterly, utterly gorgeous. Dead romantic, really mature and get this – he turns up to meet me after work on the Sunday afternoon in this brand new silver convertible.'

'So, er, how old is he?' said Hazel.

'Twenty-four.'

'Twenty-four!' screamed Hazel, as Mr Jenson walked over and stood behind them. 'Abbie, you're only sixteen.'

'Are you turning into my mother or what?' said Abbie, laughing. 'I'm *seventeen* in November and besides, Tom reckons age isn't important.'

'You've got five minutes,' Mr Jenson said, frowning at Abbie.

'Give us a hand, will you?' said Abbie, speaking to Dee for the first time. 'You've almost finished yours. I mean this is stupid. How can I have three subjects all at the same time?'

'You haven't, dozo,' said Joe. 'Look, today's Wednesday, right? So you've got English here, OK, then Music.'

He was wasting his time. Abbie had stopped listening, the minute Mr Jenson had moved away.

9

'Can't see the point, really,' Abbie whispered. 'I probably won't be around that long. I might leave at Christmas.'

'What?' said Hazel.

'Tom says sixth form and Uni's a waste of time. He says you're better off going straight into work, like he did, getting an apprenticeship or something, working your way up. So I could go into retail.'

'You mean be a shop assistant?' said Joe.

'Yeah,' said Abbie, scowling at him. 'But do a management course while I'm earning. Avoid a whole load of student debt.'

Dee listened as she and Joe filled in Abbie's timetable for her. There wasn't anything wrong with Abbie's scheme, as such, except this was a guy she'd only known for three weeks yet she was seriously thinking of changing all her plans for him! It must be love – or something dangerously close. Something that was stirring up memories. Memories of Lauren. Lauren and Dad. Stuff Dee didn't want to think about just now.

Hazel sighed as she got off the bus and began the long walk down the lane towards their farm. She was shattered. They hadn't actually done much work but she was still a bit jet-lagged, not to mention traumatised from the whole airport camping fiasco. Added to which, the first day back had been a whole lot more dramatic than she'd expected. There'd been Abbie's news for a start, then that business at lunch when Joe's little cousin, Oliver, had come rushing up to the new girl, Dee.

'Your brother's done a bunk,' he'd announced. 'I'm supposed to be looking after him but there was a bit of bother in the lunch queue. Couple of lads started pushing and Scott just ran off! Shall I tell our form teacher or what?'

Hazel had gone with Dee to intercept Scott, bring him back. Luckily he hadn't been gone long and wasn't difficult to find, as he'd been scurrying straight back to his gran's. He was a funny kid, sort of young for his age, dead sweet but a bit vacant, like he was off in his own little world.

She'd asked Dee if he was autistic or something but Dee said not and didn't seem to want to talk about it so Hazel had let it drop. Scott obviously had special needs of some sort though, 'cos they'd delivered him to Mrs Mitchell in 'the unit'. When they got back to the common room Abbie was still droning on about Tom to anyone who'd listen, while poor Sanjay had stared out of the window, trying to look as if he didn't care.

'She didn't even tell Sanjay to his face this time,' Joe had muttered. 'Sent him a text. A bloody text, can you believe that?'

Hazel couldn't. Not really. It was pretty bad. Even by Abbie's standards. And this Tom seemed a whole lot more serious than any of Abbie's other little flings. Hazel paused for a moment, adjusting the strap of her bag that was cutting into her shoulder, before tackling the short hill that led to the farm. As she turned the final corner she was greeted by a herd of cows plodding across the lane towards the milking shed, her dad at one side, their collie, Max, at the other.

'Good timing,' her dad said. 'You can close the gates for me.'

Hazel closed the field gate and, as the last of the cows passed, she saw a red Fiesta parked outside the house.

'Is Sarah here?' Hazel asked, somewhat pointlessly as the car could have hardly driven over on its own.

'Yes,' said Dad. 'She came about an hour ago.'

'With Gary?'

'No, Gary's at work,' said Dad. 'So it's just Sarah and Lucy.'

'Are they staying for dinner?'

'I don't know,' said Dad. 'I didn't know she was coming today at all. No one tells me anything,' he added, in mock exasperation.

Hazel smiled and hurried towards the house. As she opened the front door she heard crying coming from upstairs. No, not crying, screaming. Nothing else. No voices, no footsteps pacing, just the screams of a very distressed baby.

That was odd, she thought, dropping her bag on the hall floor and heading straight upstairs. Sarah never let Lucy cry like that. In fact she usually picked her up at the merest hint of a whimper. Typically anxious first-time mum, was Sarah. Hazel pushed open the door of the spare room where they kept a cot for Lucy's visits.

'Oh, sweetheart,' Hazel said, picking up her howling niece. 'Where's Mummy? Is she ignoring you? Ssshhh, now. It's all right.'

Lucy's cries quietened as her tiny fingers reached out, grasping the edge of Hazel's collar.

'Are you hungry?' Hazel asked, gently kissing Lucy's forehead and patting her back, as she'd seen Sarah do. 'Shall we go and find Mummy?'

She headed downstairs, carefully, quietly, so as not to set Lucy off crying again. There was no one in the lounge or the small sitting room at the back. Kitchen then, they must be in the kitchen. The door to the kitchen was half open and, at first, Hazel didn't think they were in there either. It was so quiet. But, as she pushed the door, she saw her sister and Mum sitting opposite each other, a letter lying between them on the table. A letter which Mum snatched up and shoved in her bag, the minute she saw Hazel.

'Er, I brought Lucy down,' said Hazel, looking from Mum to Sarah. 'She was crying.'

'Was she?' said Sarah vacantly.

13

She stood up, automatically, as though she was sleepwalking, and took Lucy from Hazel's arms.

'Is everything all right?' Hazel asked.

'Of course,' said her mum over-brightly. 'Why?'

'Nothing,' said Hazel.

She knew there was no point pushing it. She was used to Mum and Sarah with their little secrets. When Sarah was pregnant, Mum was the first to know. Even before Gary! Their closeness belonged to a time, way back, before Hazel was born, before Mum met Dad; to the six years Mum and Sarah had been on their own. A time neither of them spoke about much. Mainly it wasn't an issue. Sarah's birth dad had disappeared long ago and, as far as families went, they were fairly functional, fairly happy. Sarah and Dad got on fine. But if Sarah had a problem, it was always Mum she turned to.

What, Hazel wondered as she made herself a drink and took it up to her room, was it this time? Something pretty serious by the looks on their faces. Lucy? No, couldn't be anything to do with Lucy. Lucy looked great – if a little grumpy. Gary? Probably not. Gary was too laid-back to ever be a problem! Money? That was the most likely, by far. Money problems again. The hurriedly hidden letter was almost certainly Sarah's bank statement or some horrendous final demand. Sarah was useless with money. Especially for someone with an Economics degree!

'That's it!' Dad had told her only last month, when he found out Mum had paid Sarah's car tax for her. 'No more hand-outs!'

It had kicked off a massive row. Mum accusing Dad of being mean with Sarah 'cos she wasn't his real daughter, which was crazy and Mum knew it. Dad was practical, careful, but never, ever mean. Especially not with Sarah. When Sarah got married, it was Dad who'd suggested giving her the deposit for her first home, thinking she'd settle for a small flat. But no, Sarah had bought a three-bedroom cottage near Windermere and saddled herself with a massive mortgage despite Dad's warnings that she and Gary would never be able to afford it, with all their student debt. Not to mention running two cars and Sarah's general passion for spending.

'We'll manage,' Sarah had said.

But what if they couldn't? What if they couldn't pay the mortgage? What if they lost the house? Dad would go mental! Worries about Sarah were interrupted by the beep of Hazel's phone. It was a message from Abbie telling her to check her email. She dutifully checked only to find that Abbie had sent her some pictures of Tom.

Oh great! Just what she wanted. Having listened to Abbie going on nonstop, all day, about 'Mr Perfection', she now had to look at photos. One showed him

15

lounging against his flash car outside his family's posh hotel, which allegedly he'd be in charge of once his parents retired next year.

So rich, tall, dark and even better looking than Abbie had made out. She could sort of see the appeal. But twenty-four! Only a couple of years younger than Sarah and Gary. Positively ancient! She just hoped Abbie knew what she was doing.

2

Abbie wriggled into the new trousers that Tom had bought her and put on a white top, the one with the long sleeves. Tom didn't like her wearing short skirts and strappy stuff. He said it made her look too young and, besides, he didn't like other blokes staring at her when she was out with him, which was sort of nice 'cos Sanjay had never even noticed things like that.

Not that she'd ever gone anywhere decent with Sanjay. The school-based 'youth club' usually, where Sanjay would spend half the night playing pool with his mates and the other half playing drums with his pathetic band, leaving her hanging around with Hazel, Joe and the rest for hours on end. Taking her for granted! Well, tough for him. It was over now, completely this time. Tom was way better than Sanjay. Tom took her out for meals, to clubs, to films or even to the theatre a couple of times. Tom treated her like a grown-up.

'Abbie,' her mum shouted. 'Dinner's ready.'

Abbie glanced at the clock, grabbed her bag and hurried downstairs.

'I don't want dinner,' she informed her mother. 'I told you this morning. I'm going out.'

'You didn't say you'd be eating out,' her mother moaned.

'Well, I am.'

Her mother did one of her irritating, exaggerated sighs, then her dad pitched in.

'You won't be able to see Tom twenty-four/seven, now you're back at school,' he said.

'Duh!' said Abbie. 'I know that! I wasn't anyway. He does have to work, you know.'

'Not much, from what I can make out,' Mum said.

'Right,' said Abbie. 'Well, you can add laziness to the list of his other imaginary faults, then, can't you?'

'Don't make this into a big deal, Abbie', said Dad. 'All we're trying to say is that you can't be out till past midnight and be up for school at seven. Tell him you need to be back early.'

'As if!' Abbie muttered, as the door bell rang.

She darted out, slamming the door behind her before her parents decided to do something completely embarrassing like talk to Tom themselves. He'd only been inside their house once and it had been a disaster. Her parents, though painfully polite, had made it quite

18

clear by their constant, probing questions that they didn't like Tom.

'It's not that we don't like him,' they'd tried to say later. 'Not really. It's just, well, the age difference for a start.'

No use pointing out that there was almost eight years between her parents because that was different, of course. Mum had been all of twenty-two when she'd met Dad!

'You look great,' Tom said, opening the car door for her.

He kissed her lightly on the cheek, as he slid into the driver's seat, the touch of his lips soothing away her bad mood.

'Told you, brown eye shadow would look better than that garish muck you usually wear,' he said, gazing at her. 'More subtle, makes you look sophisticated. We're going to The Boar, by the way, meeting up with Paige and Leo.'

'Brill,' said Abbie, forcing a smile.

Paige was a twenty-three-year-old actress, albeit a 'resting' one, who was temporarily working as a waitress at Tom's hotel. Leo was her boyfriend but that hadn't stopped her flirting with Tom, each time they'd met up, which was far too often, in Abbie's opinion. The flirting wasn't the worst thing though. Tom seemed to change when he was with his friends, alternately ignoring her or putting her down. Or, maybe, she was being silly and it was just her imagination, like Tom said.

'So try not to look so much like a scared rabbit, tonight, eh?' he was saying, as he left the dual carriageway. 'Paige and Leo are OK, so relax, try to enjoy it. And don't talk about school!'

That, Abbie thought, was part of the problem. She didn't have much else to talk about but she'd try. For Tom's sake she'd try.

'I'm going down the park for a bit,' Kieran announced, as he helped Dee clear up after dinner. 'I'm meeting some mates from school.'

Mates already! People to hang out with. Not that Dee was really surprised. Kieran made friends easily and seemed as confident and outgoing as ever, as if totally untouched by what had happened. Like he'd completely ignored and opted out of the last few years. Like he'd forgotten Lauren had ever existed!

'D'yer wanna come?' he asked Scott, prompted by a nod from Dee. 'There's bound to be some lads from your year around.'

Scott shook his head and scurried upstairs to the bedroom he shared with Kieran, where he'd lose himself in the fantasy of computer games. Not the zap-pow sort but complicated simulations, building cities, populating them with families so unlike his own. It was good for him, the educational psychologist had said. He said the games gave Scott a place of security to escape to, but Dee wasn't sure that escape was the best tactic. Sooner or later Scott would have to come out of his cocoon, face things, move on, like they were all trying to do.

She wandered through to the lounge where her grandparents were reading and her dad was staring, blankly, at the TV. His face looked grey, strained, worn out. He was only forty-six but in many ways seemed older than Gran or Granddad. He looked up and smiled as she went in, giving her hope that the old Dad might suddenly return. She sat down next to him on the settee.

'So what've you been up to, today?' she asked.

He smiled again but the effort of answering seemed too great and he remained as silent as he'd been over dinner, doped up on the cocktail of pills the doctor had prescribed.

'You helped me do a bit of gardening, didn't you, Peter?' Gran said, as if talking to a small child.

Dad nodded and smiled again, like some sort of bloody robot or zombie. Not a man with a doctorate in politics, a man who'd written books, lectured to halls full of students. Dee couldn't bear it, she couldn't bear to see him reduced to this. She got up, went into the kitchen, poured herself a glass of water. As she drank, she became aware that someone had followed her. She turned to see Granddad standing by the door.

'He'll be all right you know,' Granddad said. 'He'll get better. People do.'

'Not while he's still blaming himself,' Dee said.

'The counselling should help with that.'

'It's not helping though, is it?' said Dee.

They'd tried everything. Psychologists, psychiatrists, support groups, individual counselling, family counselling. Nothing worked. It had been one of the family counsellors who'd suggested that they moved away from Liverpool, from the house, the memories. It had seemed sensible to move near to Dad's parents and planning the move had definitely perked Dad up a bit. So much so that he'd applied for jobs, sailed through his very first interview and been accepted to teach at a college. But the improvement hadn't lasted. By August he'd relapsed into total depression, had to pull out of the job before he'd even started it, so now Gran was trying to get a different kind of therapy fixed up and the temporary arrangement of staying with them was beginning to look increasingly permanent.

Not that living here bothered Dee. It took some of the pressure off her and she'd always got on well with her grandparents, who were both in their early seventies and mercifully in good health. But it couldn't be easy for them. Hardly ideal. Instead of travelling, going on the cruises they'd planned, enjoying their retirement, they'd been lumbered with a whole load of trouble and, despite

Granddad's upbeat message, Dee knew he was worried. It had been almost two years now but neither Dad nor Scott were getting much better.

'Give it time, Dee,' Granddad was saying.

Dee nodded before heading upstairs to check on Scott. Maybe time was the problem, she thought as she stood in Scott's doorway, watching him clicking away at his mouse, building fantasies. Because, in Dad's case certainly, it wasn't only what had happened two years ago, it was what had gone on before. Years of trauma she'd barely been aware of, barely understood, gradually building up, waiting to explode. Why hadn't she noticed? How could she have been so utterly blind?

'People don't always notice the signs,' one of the counsellors had tried to tell her. 'And, if they do, they misinterpret them. You were only children. You couldn't be expected to know!'

The mere thought of it all made Dee shudder. She went into her own room, the tiny one at the back of the house, turned up the heater, sat down on the bed and picked up a picture from the bedside table. One of the few photographs from her early childhood that were left, that hadn't been destroyed. This one had been taken at Knowsley Safari Park.

It showed her, in the foreground, balancing on the back of Kieran's pushchair, Dad's arms wrapped round her to stop her falling, Mum standing close by. The four of them together. Five if you counted Scott, visible only as a very large bulge in Mum's stomach. So who had taken the photo? One of her grandparents, perhaps? A passing stranger? She couldn't remember. She couldn't remember much about that day at all. Even worse, she couldn't remember much about Mum. It was as if all the memories had been wiped out, destroyed along with the photographs. Or had they just been replaced by memories of someone else? Of *her*. Lauren. Someone Dee would much rather forget.

Dee stared at the photo, trying to think about Mum, what they'd done that day, how they'd felt. It must have been a good day. They all looked happy, anyway. Mum was smiling, relaxed, confident. Why shouldn't she be? She had no idea, did she? That in eighteen months her life would be over, wiped out by a couple of drunken teenagers driving a stolen car. Dee felt the familiar pain tighten across her ribs, the pain that was more like anger than loss. If Mum hadn't gone to see her friend that night, if those lads hadn't stolen that car, if Mum hadn't died then Dad would never have got involved with Lauren, would he? None of this would have happened.

Dee slammed the photograph down. What was the point? She was supposed to be moving on, not looking back. She got her folder out of her bag, almost wishing she had homework to do, something that would tire her out, help her to sleep. It would be better next week when term really got underway. She stared at her timetable trying to remember the rooms, the corridors, the layout of the school and the bewildering number of new people she'd met – Hazel, Abbie – you couldn't really forget Abbie! Her poor ex, Sanjay. Joe, with his funny moustache. Sean, Tasha and dozens of others who she could just about picture but whose names she couldn't remember.

People who seemed to have known each other for ever! Luckily they didn't seem too cliquey though. Most of them had been dead friendly, keen to get her involved and she'd signed up for a whole load of clubs, activities, things to keep her busy. Hazel and Joe had even persuaded her to sign up for badminton on Wednesdays after school.

'I don't think so,' Dee had protested, at first. 'I'm hopeless at sport.'

'Good,' said Hazel. 'With any luck you'll be worse than me, so Sanjay'll have someone else to yell at for a change. He's the C team coach,' Hazel had explained. 'A complete sports freak. But don't worry, it's not like serious yelling. It's just joking.'

Hazel had paused, looking over at Abbie.

'Don't expect Abbie'll turn up this year. Pity. You should see her trying to play without ruffling her hair or breaking her nails! It's a right laugh.'

Everything, as far as Dee could tell, was a laugh to Hazel and Abbie. They were just the kind of friends she needed.

Hazel lay in bed, listening to the voices coming from the lounge. Sarah had decided to stay the night, which was odd because she hadn't been drinking or anything. In fact she'd hardly eaten either. Neither had Mum but that wasn't so unusual 'cos Mum had vowed to go on one of her many diets once the holiday was over. They'd sat, at dinner, talking about fairly ordinary things. Sarah asking Hazel about her first day back, laughing at Hazel's impersonation of Abbie rambling on about her great romance.

It would have been hard to tell that anything was wrong at all except that Sarah looked a bit pale and both she and Mum kept glancing at the clock. Dad had gone to bed early, as usual, at ten. Hazel had got the hint and gone up minutes later, leaving Sarah alone with Mum. Pity they'd chosen to sit in the lounge, directly below her bedroom, because they were keeping her awake. Over an hour now they'd been talking!

Not that Hazel could hear anything useful. The odd word drifted up occasionally. She thought she'd heard her name a couple of times. She heard it again. Why? Why were they talking about her? She got out of bed, walked across the room, cursing the creaking floorboards, and opened the door. She crept to the top of the stairs, descending quietly until almost at the bottom. The lounge door was closed but she could hear them fairly clearly.

'I think you're right,' Mum was saying. 'It's best not to tell anyone else yet. Well, maybe Gary. But not your dad and certainly not Hazel.'

Why? What could be all right for Gary to know but not her or Dad? Hazel moved closer to the lounge. She knew she shouldn't be doing this, shouldn't be listening in but she couldn't help it. She'd always been the same. Even as a kid, learning the terrible truth about Santa by hovering at the top of the stairs when she should have been in bed.

'Maybe we won't ever have to tell them,' said Sarah. 'It might, well, it might not be as serious as we think.'

That was Sarah. Constantly living in a blissful state of denial. Whatever troubles, whatever debts she got herself into, she always believed it would sort itself out.

'No,' said Mum. 'We'll have a better idea next week, when we see the consultant.'

Consultant! They were seeing a financial consultant! It must be bad. No wonder Sarah didn't want Dad to find out.

'So I'll pick you up about nine o'clock on Tuesday morning,' Sarah was saying.

'What about Lucy?' Mum said.

27

'Well, Gary'll be working, so I could leave her with Dad, I suppose. Tell him we're going shopping. Or maybe I could take her with me. She's no trouble.'

'I know,' said Mum. 'But I never think hospitals are right for babies. You never know what they might pick up.'

Hospitals? Consultants. Medical consultant not financial consultant! But why? Sarah wasn't ill, was she? And she surely couldn't be pregnant again? Not so soon.

'Yeah, you're right,' said Sarah, yawning loudly enough for Hazel to hear from behind the closed door.

'You'd better get to bed,' Mum said. 'You look shattered.'

'Yeah well, it's all been a bit of shock but,' Sarah added, lightening her tone, 'it'll be all right. You'll see!'

The movement, the sound of cups being picked up, made Hazel bolt back to her bedroom. She'd just got back into bed when she heard Sarah walk past and go into the next room. The farmhouse walls were thick but Hazel could hear her sister moving round, getting ready for bed. There was something else too, something other than the movement. Crying, Sarah was crying. Softly, like she was trying to hold it in, like she was scared someone might hear.

Hazel sat up. Should she go in? Despite the ten-year age gap and the fact that they had different birth dads, she and Sarah were close. They even looked quite similar, both of them taking after Mum: shortish, not fat but not exactly super-slim either, with wide mouths and slightly squashed noses, which made them look 'interesting' rather than pretty. They got on well too, usually, but only in their accepted roles. Sarah was 'big sister', the one who offered advice or comfort, not the one who took it. Would Sarah tell her what was wrong or get mad at her for listening in?

Words from the conversation started to come back to her. 'Bit of a shock.' 'Consultant.' This wasn't a GP they were seeing. It had got further than that. Something serious? Something to do with having Lucy? The birth hadn't exactly been easy. Sarah had ended up having a Caesarean. It had gone well, allegedly. But could there have been some side effect, some complication? Something so scary it would make Sarah cry?

No way could she wait till next week to find out. She swung her legs over the side of the bed. Got up. She started to move towards the door but the crying had stopped. It was quiet, totally quiet. Maybe Sarah had cried herself to sleep. Maybe it was best not to ask Sarah at all. Mum. Mum was the one to tackle. Tomorrow. Tomorrow morning, once Sarah had gone.

3

On Thursday morning Dee got up early, as she always did, so she could use the bathroom in peace. She'd showered, dressed and had just got back to her bedroom when there was a sharp knock on the door.

'Yes,' she said, looking up as Kieran slouched in, hands in pockets, head down.

'Er,' he said. 'You couldn't lend us a couple of quid, could you?'

'Why? What for?'

'Lunch.'

'Gran gave us lunch money, yesterday.'

'I lost it.'

'Well use your paper-round money then.'

'Can't,' said Keiran. 'That's gone too. Think my wallet must have fell out of my pocket. In the park or summat.'

The mention of the park, the way Kieran was avoiding her gaze, alerted Dee.

'You've spent it all, haven't you?' she accused.

'No!'

'Kieran,' she said, a little less fiercely. 'It's not dope again, is it? You haven't been buying more dope?'

'No!'

'You said you were gonna quit all that,' said Dee, 'when we left Liverpool.'

'I know!' said Kieran. 'And I have.'

'Please don't start again, Kieran,' she pleaded. 'Gran and Granddad have got enough to worry about without you kicking off. They'd go ballistic if they ever found out you'd been mucking about with drugs. And the last thing Dad needs is more stress.'

'Are you listening or what?' Kieran snapped. 'I'm not doing no drugs, right! I lost my wallet, that's all. Came to you 'cos I didn't want to take no more money off Gran. Now are you gonna lend me some or what?'

Did she believe him? Dee wasn't sure. Kieran had been barely thirteen when he'd started on dope but he didn't seem to think it was any big deal. Said it just helped him 'chill'. Dee hadn't told her dad or anyone. What was the point? They'd all been so wrapped up with Scott, with the other business. But with a mixture of bribery and threats, she'd managed to persuade Kieran to stop. Or at least she hoped she had. Maybe Kieran wasn't as in control, as unaffected by stuff, as he liked to make out.

'There's a fiver in the front of that small bag,' said

Dee, nodding towards the bedside table. 'Make it last till the weekend.'

As Dee brushed her hair, she realised Kieran was still hovering by the table. She swung round, ready to snap at him for rummaging in the bag, taking more than a fiver, playing with her phone or whatever he was doing. But the bag had been thrown onto the bed and the thing in Kieran's hand wasn't her mobile, it was a photograph, the one taken at Knowsley.

'How did he cope then? Dad? After Mum died?' Kieran asked.

Dee looked at him, wondering what he was up to. It wasn't like Kieran to talk about feelings, personal stuff.

'Well, I was only little,' Kieran added, defensively. 'Don't really remember, do I? I mean did he get ... was he like ... how he is now?'

'No,' she said, sitting down on the edge of the bed. 'I don't think so. I mean, he changed, I guess. We all did, I suppose. But he got through it. Dad's not a weak person, Kieran,' she added.

'Never said he was.'

'No, but I reckon that's what you think, sometimes,' she said, feeling her shoulders tighten in irrational anger. 'But he's not. It wasn't easy for him, after Mum died. With us being so young and everything. Fitting work round us. Organising friends and neighbours to help out the rest of the time.'

She was deliberately focusing on the practical stuff, avoiding reference to how clingy Scott had been, to Kieran's wild tantrums, to her own bewildered, quiet withdrawal, which had probably worried Dad most of all. Things it was just too painful, too pointless to revisit.

'And we had that nanny for a while,' she went on, 'until Scott started nursery. Remember her?'

'Not really. Sort of,' Kieran mumbled. 'And did Dad have, you know, any girlfriends before . . .'

'Don't think so,' said Dee. 'Don't remember any. No, I'm pretty sure he didn't. There was only . . .'

'Lauren,' said Kieran.

'Yeah, her,' said Dee, sharply, as a picture of Lauren immediately lodged in her mind. 'Why? Why all the questions all of a sudden?'

'Dunno,' said Kieran. 'I think about it sometimes. About her – you know? Try not to. But you can't help it, can you?'

'You're doing well if you only think about her *some* of the time,' said Dee. 'I never stop.'

Hazel stood, holding Lucy, hoping she wasn't going to puke or dribble down the front of her school shirt.

'Thanks,' said Sarah, packing up the last of Lucy's baby stuff into a large bag. 'Do you want a lift to school? I don't mind driving round that way. Be quite handy. I could call at the supermarket on the way back.'

33

It wasn't quite what Hazel had in mind. She'd hoped to get a few minutes alone with Mum before setting off to catch the bus but a glance at the clock told her there wasn't time. So maybe she should change plans again. Take the lift. Ask Sarah outright what was going on last night. Risk being told to mind her own business.

'Yeah, OK, thanks,' she said, as she watched Sarah hug Mum a little too tightly, too intensely. 'A lift would be good.'

The journey to school, by bus, took for ever, stopping at every hamlet, every group of houses but, by car, it would only take about fifteen minutes. Not much time for conversation. Best to be direct.

'Sarah,' she began, as soon as they pulled out of the yard. 'Is everything OK?'

'Yeah, 'course. Why?'

'I heard you crying, last night.'

'It was probably Lucy.'

'And I heard you talking to Mum – about going to the hospital.'

'Oh,' said Sarah.

Hazel waited for Sarah to go on, to break the silence.

'We weren't going to tell you,' Sarah said, eventually.

'I gathered that.'

'I mean, there didn't seem any point,' said Sarah. 'Worrying everybody before we really knew anything definite. You know what Dad's like for flapping. And we didn't want you getting all upset over something that might not turn out to be anything much.'

'Sarah, I'm almost seventeen. I'm not a kid! Whatever it turns out to be, I want to know. You're my sister, for heaven's sake. If you're ill, if there's something wrong, I want to know!'

Sarah suddenly pulled into a lay-by, switched off the engine.

'It's not me,' she said, turning round. 'There's nothing wrong with me, Hazel. It's Mum.'

'Guess why I was late this morning?' said Joe, as a group of them took advantage of their sixth form freedom to walk into town at lunchtime.

For a moment, no one answered. Hazel was thinking about Mum. About what Sarah had said. Having to concentrate on each step because her legs felt weak and her head was throbbing. Everyone else was huddled round Abbie's mobile, looking at fuzzy pictures of Tom.

'I dunno,' said Hazel, eventually feeling obliged to make an effort. 'Why?'

'I went for my driving test,' said Joe.

'Driving test! You never said! And?'

'I passed.'

Dee and Tasha, who'd obviously been a little less involved in the photographs than the others, turned round.

'Wow!' Tasha said. 'Congratulations. First time?'

'Yeah,' said Joe, as everyone else tuned in. 'But it's no big deal,' he added, modestly. 'Been driving since I was a kid, 'aven't I? Quads, tractors and stuff.'

'Still pretty impressive,' said Abbie, putting her phone away. 'First in our year to pass! Why didn't you tell us earlier?'

'I didn't get a chance with you gibbering on about Tom all morning.'

'Whoops, sorry,' said Abbie. 'But I've just got to tell you about his amazing...'

'Anyway,' Joe interrupted. 'Mum says I can borrow her car on Saturday if anyone fancies going bowling.'

'Yeah,' said Sean. 'I'm up for it. But we're not all going to squeeze into your mum's Ka, are we?'

'I'll ask Sanjay,' said Joe. 'He can take four in his Corsa. And Tom drives, so...'

'Tom?' said Abbie. 'Go bowling? With us? He won't – I mean, I – he's working Saturday night.'

'OK,' said Joe. 'Well, I guess you won't want go with Sanjay, so I'll pick you up around seven.'

'No,' said Abbie. 'I can't.'

'Why not?' said Joe. 'If Tom's working, what's the problem?'

'There isn't one,' said Abbie. 'Except he sometimes phones me in his break.'

'So talk to him from the bowling alley!'

'I can't. Not properly,' said Abbie, 'not with all the noise and everything.'

'So you'd rather stay in?' said Joe. 'On the off chance of getting a five-minute call from Tom, rather than go out with us? Well, that puts us in our place, doesn't it?'

'Yep!' said Abbie. 'Sure does. Anyway it might keep Mum and Dad off my back if I stay in and pretend to do a bit of homework or something.'

'Fine,' said Joe. 'Enjoy it. I'll take Tasha then. Sanjay can pick Dee up. Hazel? Hello! Earth calling Hazel.'

'What? Sorry,' said Hazel, as she felt a gentle nudge in her ribs.

She'd been aware of the conversation. Thought she'd been listening properly. But she couldn't have been. Somehow the voices had blurred and she'd been back in that lay-by listening to another voice. Sarah's voice.

'Don't tell me you don't want to come neither,' Joe was moaning.

'Me? Yeah,' Hazel muttered. 'Sure. I'll come.'

'Act normally,' Sarah had said. 'Don't let Mum or Dad see you're upset. Just keep it to yourself for a few days, eh, until we've seen the doctor on Tuesday.'

It had made a certain sort of sense, when Sarah had said it. But already it seemed impossible. She wanted to tell someone. Talk to someone. Abbie. Abbie was who she talked to about personal things. OK, it was always a bit risky with Abbie's big mouth and everything but they'd been sharing secrets from infant school so it seemed sort of natural somehow. Except now Abbie was totally wrapped up with Tom. As if to prove the point, Abbie had got her phone again and was trying to interest Joe in her photos.

Hazel hung back a few paces. She could tell Joe. Joe was a good listener. Better than Abbie in many ways and certainly less likely to blab. Or maybe she could just phone Sarah. She got her phone out, put it away again. As she got it out for the second time, she happened to glance across the road, where a small figure was darting behind a tree, trying to hide. Hazel hurried forward, caught up with the others and tapped Dee's arm.

'Er, I think your brother's escaped again,' she said.

'Oh shit,' said Dee, immediately darting across the road towards Scott.

Hazel hesitated for a moment, then followed.

'Hey, Scott, what you doing?' Dee was asking.

'Going home.'

'Why? What's happened this time? Has someone been bothering you?'

Scott shook his head.

'What then?'

'It's PE this afternoon.'

'That's OK,' Dee said. 'We sorted all that, remember?'

'Yes,' said Scott. 'But Jamie Smith says everyone's got to do it.'

'Well, Jamie Smith's wrong,' said Dee firmly. 'Have you got your note?'

Scott nodded.

'Good,' said Dee. 'And I'll even remind Mr Jenson in registration, OK?'

Scott still didn't look convinced. As they began to walk back with him towards school, Hazel wondered why he couldn't do PE. He was a bit odd, admittedly, but he looked fine physically. He was breathing all right; no hint of asthma or anything like that. Epilepsy, maybe? But even that wouldn't stop you doing games, would it?

'Have you had lunch?' Dee was asking him.

Scott shook his head.

Hazel rummaged in her pocket for the bar of chocolate she'd bought as comfort food at break then decided not to eat. Maybe that would cheer Scott up a touch. As she pulled it out, offered it to him, Scott's eyes widened and he leapt back, crashing into Dee.

'Jeez!' said Hazel. 'Sorry. I mean, is he allergic or something?'

'Sudden movements,' said Dee, as if that explained everything. 'Go on, Scott, it's OK. Have the chocolate.'

Hazel offered it again, slowly this time and Scott took it.

'Thanks,' he said, his face suddenly relaxing, looking almost normal.

Hazel, despite her own worries, found herself

wanting to hug him but thought better of it, not least because he might bite! He was such a strange little thing, there was no telling what he might do.

By the time they'd got Scott safely settled, there didn't seem much point in going into town so they bought sandwiches from the canteen and sat outside in one of the quadrangles.

'So what's the deal with PE?' Hazel asked. 'Why can't he do it?'

'He's on a sort of special educational programme,' said Dee, looking at her feet. 'He's only in class for a couple of subjects. Spends the rest of the time in the unit. He's not thick or anything. Dead bright, really. But he's missed a fair bit of school and . . . '

'Joe missed a year,' said Hazel, trying to fill the awkward silence as Dee's voice trailed. 'That's why he's a bit older than the rest of our class. He got meningitis in his last year at juniors. It really knocked him back.'

She paused, hoping the revelations about Joe's illness might prompt something more about Scott.

'He really likes you, doesn't he?' said Dee.

'Who?'

'Joe!'

'Yeah, well I told you, we're mates. He's been in my class since we started seniors and our parents are friends, so yeah, we're pretty close, I guess.'

'I meant likes as in fancies.'

'Mm, maybe,' said Hazel. 'I've never really thought of Joe in that way. Though Sarah reckons she's noticed a change recently. In the way Joe acts around me.'

'Sarah?'

'Er, my sister,' said Hazel, a wave of sickness surging through her stomach, as she remembered Sarah's face, totally white, the hands trembling on the steering wheel as she'd continued the drive to school.

'And Sarah reckons Joe fancies you too, right? Hazel? Are you OK? I'm sorry. Did I say the wrong thing?'

'No,' said Hazel. 'It's nothing to do with Joe. Or you. I was just thinking about summat.'

She paused. Looked at Dee. Should she tell her? No. She couldn't. It was hardly the sort of thing you blurted out to someone you'd only known a couple of days. Besides, it looked like Dee had enough problems of her own.

'Abbie,' Hazel said. 'I was thinking about Abbie. And Tom.'

'Mmm,' said Dee, quietly. 'Seems pretty besotted. Hope she's gonna be OK. Tom sounds a bit sort of – creepy.'

'Creepy?' said Hazel, forcing a smile. 'Are you kidding? Sounds too flaming perfect to me.'

'That's what I mean,' said Dee, quietly.

4

'Abbie, are you up yet? I've been calling you! It's turned half past seven.'

Abbie groaned and pulled the duvet over her head. She didn't care what time it was. The duvet was whipped away and Abbie looked up to see her mother hovering over her.

'You'll be late for school,' her mother snapped.

School. Monday. Oh no, it was Monday morning already. The weekend was over. Impossible!

'I've got a headache,' Abbie began.

Big mistake.

'Haven't we all?' said her mother. 'Waiting up for you until four o'clock this morning!'

'You didn't have to wait up. I phoned. At least three times. I told you where I was.'

'Four o'clock!' her mother went on, ignoring her. 'It's outrageous to be staying out that late when it's work and school the next day. And you *are* going to school,

Abbie. No matter how many headaches you've got. So get yourself up right now. I want you downstairs in five minutes. We need to talk.'

'I thought we just had,' Abbie muttered, as she slithered out of bed and lurched towards the bathroom.

She brushed her teeth, rubbing at her tongue with her toothbrush. She hadn't really drunk that much but it felt as though she had. Looked like it too, with her skin dull and her eyes slightly bloodshot. Had somebody been tampering with her drinks or what? Feeling slightly sick, dizzy, she had a quick shower and washed her hair. No time to dry it so she dressed and pulled her hair up into a ponytail. That was the great thing about long hair. It was easy, versatile. She wrapped it round into a tight knot and stuck some hairgrips in. She'd read somewhere that grips were fashionable again. Besides, it didn't matter. It was only school. It wasn't like she was going to bump into Tom or anything.

'Abbie, I said five minutes,' her mum yelled from downstairs.

'Right!' said Abbie, abandoning her usual make-up routine in favour of just a quick touch of lip gloss and mascara.

Pretty basic but it would have to do. She fixed what she hoped was a suitably contrite look on her face and went down to the kitchen.

'I'm sorry,' she said, hoping to head off the worst of the trouble. 'I mean, I didn't know Tom's car was going to break down, did I?'

'The car broke down at midnight, allegedly,' her dad said. 'So what took so long? Why didn't you do as we said and get a taxi home?'

Did he know? Had he guessed that the whole thing was a pack of lies? That the car hadn't broken down at all? That she'd been miles away from home when she'd realised how late she was going to be – too far to get a taxi.

'Taxis were all booked,' she said. 'Besides I didn't think it'd take so long to fix the car. Not at first. Anyway, chill, will you? It was a one-off. It won't happen again.'

'Certainly not this week,' her mum said, 'because you're grounded.'

'Don't be stupid!' Abbie yelled. 'Like I'm supposed to tell Tom I'm grounded, yeah? Like some bloody kid.'

'I don't care what you tell him,' said her mother, 'but you're not going out this week.'

'I'll do what I like,' said Abbie, picking up her bag, pushing past her mum. 'You can't stop me.'

'Abbie, what about your breakfast?' said Dad, putting tea and toast on the table.

'Stuff your bloody breakfast,' Abbie called, as she stormed out, slamming the door.

Despite Mum's moans about lateness, Abbie was ages early at the bus stop and it had started to rain. There was no shelter, so she moved down the road a bit and huddled in the doorway of the local bakery, imagining the conversation going on at home. Mum would probably be crying or something. Overreacting as usual!

'I don't know what's happening to Abbie,' Dad would be saying. 'She never used to be like this. Not until she met this Tom.'

'Why couldn't she have stuck with Sanjay?' Mum would chip in. 'He's such a nice lad.'

Life was definitely simpler with Sanjay: that was for sure. His parents were even more painfully old-fashioned than hers and Sanjay was pretty boring really so the question of staying out late never arose. It was sort of accepted that they'd be home by half ten, with wild extensions on Fridays and Saturdays. Just how the hell was she supposed to start training her parents to fit in with Tom's lifestyle?

Or maybe she needn't bother. What she'd told them was right, wasn't it? They couldn't actually stop her going out, could they? They weren't going to physically restrain her or barricade the doors, were they? OK, so they might cut off her allowance but even that didn't matter. Not with Tom insisting on paying for everything. She didn't need lifts from her parents any more either. Didn't need anything from them, really. Tom was more than just a boyfriend. Tom was freedom.

Dee yawned as she watched Scott go off into the junior playground. He wasn't too bad this morning, considering he'd had one of his nightmares again. The really terrible sort where he woke the whole house with his screams. Dee had been the first out of bed, the first to find him outside the bathroom door, pointing, his eyes wide and his hand shaking. She hadn't touched him. They knew not to touch him when he was sleepwalking. Instead she'd talked to him, quietly, until her voice filtered through his subconscious and the screams subsided into whimpers. Gran had taken over then, guiding Scott back to his room where she'd sat with him until he fell back to sleep.

As Dee watched Scott huddle against the wall in the corner of the playground, his new mate, Oliver, bounded over to him and, to her relief, Scott smiled. He seemed fairly relaxed. More relaxed than her, probably! As she moved towards the door, she gently rubbed her bruised finger. The one she'd hurt at the bowling alley on Saturday night. But it wasn't the finger that was really the problem. The problem was Sanjay.

He'd been fairly quiet on the way to the bowling alley. Concentrating on his driving, she'd guessed. Then when they arrived they'd separated, naturally, into two groups. Sanjay had been in the other lane with the serious bowlers while she, Joe and one of Joe's loopy mates played it for laughs. Hazel had been in their lane too but she hadn't really been into it. In fact, she'd given up after the first game and seemed to have spent half the night on the phone to her sister.

Dee had found herself glancing over to the other lane from time to time, watching Sanjay, admiring his style – the intense look of concentration as he rolled the ball, that amazing smile every time he got a strike. She could see why a girl like Abbie had gone for him. He was easily the best-looking lad in the whole school: the sort who managed to be good at everything but cool and popular at the same time. Totally sick-making if he hadn't been so flaming nice as well! He'd wandered over at one point, guided her arm, so she actually hit a couple of skittles, for once. Then in the coffee bar, later, Sanjay had examined her injured finger, holding on to her hand for rather a long time, reassuring her that the finger definitely wasn't broken.

He'd driven her home, dropped her last, despite advice from the others that it would be quicker to drop her first. They'd sat in the car, chatting, trying to ignore Kieran being a prat, staring down at them from the bedroom window, pulling stupid faces until he'd got bored and disappeared. Sanjay had talked a fair bit about Abbie. Nothing too deep, too personal. It was just that every single topic of conversation seemed to involve Abbie's name.

Dee had been so sure Sanjay was still hooked on Abbie that she was totally unprepared for what happened when she was about to get out of the car. Sanjay had leant over and kissed her! Not a quick peck but a proper full on kiss. And she'd responded! Could barely help responding. It had just felt right somehow, natural, sort of better than when she'd kissed other guys.

'See ya then,' Sanjay had said, as the lingering kiss ended.

Just that. He hadn't asked her out or promised to phone. Hadn't even asked for her number or looked at her as she got out of the car. So maybe she hadn't quite measured up to Abbie in the kissing stakes. She certainly couldn't measure up to Abbie in any other way. Who could? So maybe Sanjay had just acted on impulse and immediately regretted it. Either way she didn't much fancy seeing him today. How was she supposed to act? What was she supposed to say? What if he blanked her completely?

She needn't have worried. As she tried to slip, unnoticed, into the common room, Sanjay appeared at her side, like he'd been waiting for her.

'How's the finger?' he said.

'It's fine,' she said but her words were drowned by a louder voice, coming from the circle of chairs to their left.

'So Tom's friend, Paige, she's an actress, right? And she had this audition, see, in Manchester on Sunday afternoon,' Abbie was telling almost everyone in the room. 'So I thought we were just gonna like wait for her then drive home. But, by the time they'd finished, Tom was hungry so we went to this fantastic restaurant and Tom ordered champagne because Paige was in tears after the shitty way she'd been treated at the auditions.'

Champagne. Lauren. The connection in Dee's head was instant, the image it conjured so overwhelming that she started to sway and had to grab Sanjay's arm to keep herself steady as Abbie went on.

'See, Tom says champagne's a waste when you're all happy already. Tom says you should drink champagne when you're on a downer.'

Champagne. Did Abbie have to keep saying it, stressing it like that? Couldn't she talk about something else? *Champagne. Lauren. That awful New Year's Day, two years ago.* Dee shook her head, tried to focus, tune in to the rest of Abbie's story, shake away the memories of Lauren – at least for a while.

'And it worked,' Abbie was squealing, ''cos like Paige got totally hyper. Insisted we go on to a club afterwards. Paige is a member of this place and it's like just so brill! Full of actors and footballers and stuff.'

She rattled off the names of half a dozen D list celebrities who Paige allegedly knew.

'None of them were there last night,' Abbie admitted. 'But get this! Leo – that's Paige's bloke – he went off to the loo and Tom was dancing with Paige, so I phone my parents with some story about why I'm gonna be so late and then I'm like just sitting there, looking around, and guess who I saw at the bar?'

After a million or so wrong guesses by her enthusiastic audience, Abbie triumphantly announced the name.

'You know!' Abbie said, as everyone stared, blankly. 'She's a model. She's been on TV, on one of the reality shows. She was the one who got chucked out for punching that other girl. Hazel, you remember, don't you? We watched it together. It was a right laugh! Hazel, come on, wake up. You've been in a total grump all morning.'

'I'm not in a grump,' said Hazel, standing up. 'I'm just pissed off with listening to you all the time! So why don't you shut the fuck up!'

There was silence for a moment, broken by the slamming of the door as Hazel stormed out.

'Blimey,' Sanjay whispered, squeezing Dee's hand. 'What was that about? I've never seen Hazel blow up at Abbie before. And she never usually swears. Not like that!'

Dee looked over to Abbie who was shrugging, smiling, trying not to look fazed.

'Hey,' said Abbie, getting up, coming towards them.

Dee instinctively pulled her hand away from Sanjay and he drifted off.

'Er, sorry,' Dee said, looking down at her hand. 'We were, er, just talking.'

'Chill,' Abbie said. 'If you and Sanjay want to get together that's fine.'

'We don't,' said Dee. 'I mean we're not. Not really.'

'Mmm,' said Abbie, 'probably just his pathetic attempt to try and make me jealous. He just can't get it through his thick skull that we're not getting back together. Not this time.'

Dee tried to suppress the blush that was creeping up her neck. How could she have been so stupid? Abbie was right. That was obviously what Sanjay was about. He didn't really fancy her at all!

'Anyway,' Abbie was saying. 'I didn't come over to talk about Sanjay. Someone told me you were after a part-time job.'

'Yeah,' said Dee. 'I've been doing some work on a caravan site over summer but they don't need me now the season's almost finished.'

'Right,' said Abbie. 'Well, there's a job going at the café soon. I'm quitting. I'll give 'em your number if

51

you like. Pay's not bad though the manageress is a bit of an old cow.'

'Is that why you're leaving?'

'No, I can handle her! It's Tom. He doesn't really like me working there. 'Cos my shifts don't fit in with his so with me being back at school it means we hardly see each other.'

'Oh, right,' said Dee, trying to shake away a thought, a comparison.

A comparison she shouldn't be making, didn't want to make. But one that seemed to leap to her mind every time Abbie mentioned Tom.

'And it's not like I need the money,' said Abbie.

'Lucky you,' said Dee.

'Well, Tom's just like sooo generous.'

Dee looked around, desperate for someone to rescue her, as Abbie unbuttoned the top of her shirt to display the gold chain Tom had bought her. Presents. Expensive presents. Another comparison, another similarity, another memory of Lauren that made Dee shiver. Mercifully the bell went before Abbie could go into details of price and, as they were making their way out, they bumped into Joe.

'What's happened with Hazel? Someone said there was some trouble,' he added, looking accusingly at Abbie. 'And now I can't find her. Can you see if she's in the loo?'

'Can't,' said Abbie. 'I've got my singing lesson.'

'Yeah, OK,' said Joe, as Abbie walked off. 'Don't put yourself out!'

'I'll go,' said Dee.

Hazel splashed cold water over her face, stood up straight, shook the water off, tried to breathe deeply. She felt sick but she couldn't go home. Couldn't let her parents know anything was wrong. All she had to do was hold on until tomorrow afternoon, until after the hospital visit.

'Mum's not actually ill,' Sarah had insisted a dozen times over the weekend. 'It's just a routine check, that's all. They have to do it, don't they?'

Mum, it seemed, had been for the first routine test before the holiday. A test no one had even known about, that Mum hadn't bothered to mention because she'd been so certain, so confident, that it would come back clear. But it hadn't. When Mum got home there'd been a letter waiting, saying they'd picked up a slight anomaly, asking Mum to come in for further checks.

'Mum was a bit freaked,' Sarah had explained. 'I mean, so was I, at first. But I re-read the letter and looked up some stuff on the net and this is pretty common. It doesn't always mean anything. It can even be a fault on the machine sometimes, a misreading, anything! There's nothing to worry about, Hazel, honestly.'

Hazel had nodded, leaving Sarah to her denial, knowing it was the only way Sarah could ever get through the next couple of days. But what if Sarah was wrong? What if it wasn't a false alarm? What if Mum was really ill? How would Sarah cope? How would any of them cope?

She turned off the tap, dabbing her face with a rough paper towel, trying to dab away the thoughts, the pictures, that had been torturing her all weekend. Images of hospitals, scans, operations and worse. Far worse. Feeling the fear, the emptiness. The sheer impossibility of life without – stop! Don't go there. Not again. No point. It wasn't going to happen. Hazel turned as she heard the door open, saw Dee and, beyond her, hovering on the corridor, was Joe.

'You OK?' Dee asked.

'Yeah fine,' said Hazel.

'You sure?' Joe said as they headed towards the form room.

'Yeah,' said Hazel. 'Just tired, that's all and the mention of Tom's name for the millionth time made me want to puke.'

'Know what you mean,' said Joe but he was looking at her quizzically, intently, like he knew she was lying.

Part of her was desperate to tell him, to tell someone, anyone, but the other part decided it would be best to wait. On Wednesday morning, once they'd had the all clear, she'd be able to explain to her friends, apologise to Abbie, set things straight. It would all be OK. Just like Sarah said.

It had to be. Anything else was unthinkable.

5

On Wednesday, after school, Dee stood on the edge of the playground, waiting for Scott. Kieran said she should let him walk home alone but she didn't want to risk it. It had been a good week so far. Scott had stayed in school. He was settling quite well, according to Mrs Mitchell. So where the heck was he? Almost everyone had come out. Most of the buses had gone. Surely she hadn't missed him?

'Don't suppose you've seen Scott?' she called out, as she saw Abbie hurrying down the drive.

'No, sorry,' Abbie shouted back. 'Gotta go. Tom's picking me up.'

Dee watched Abbie's retreating figure, hoping to catch a glimpse of the mysterious Tom but they'd obviously arranged to meet away from the school. Considering Abbie talked about Tom so much, she didn't seem keen to show him off in person. No one, as far as Dee knew, had actually met him yet. Not even

Hazel. Hazel! Someone else to worry about. Hazel hadn't been in school today and no one seemed to know why. What's more, Abbie hadn't seemed to care.

'Bug, I expect. Might explain why she was so ratty again yesterday. Having a go at me for no reason,' Abbie had said, before steering the conversation back to Tom.

Why did every mention of Tom, every word meant as gushing praise, remind Dee of . . . She shook her head, trying to get rid of the idea before it took hold again. Tom was probably nothing like that! Tom was probably perfectly ordinary, nice, sane, normal. But the way Abbie talked obsessively about him, the way he'd totally taken over her life; that definitely reminded her of something.

The something that started about three years after Mum died, when Dad began coming home a bit later from work, relaxed, smiling, with the name 'Lauren' increasingly dropped into conversations.

'Sorry,' Dad said one night when he picked them up from a neighbour later than ever. 'I got talking to that new lady, Lauren, in the bursar's office, again. It's her birthday on Sunday. I said I'd take her out for a meal but Lauren said she'd rather come round here, meet you lot. Must be mad, eh? So what do you reckon? Shall we make her a cake?'

The cake was gross. It was supposed to be a sponge but they'd used the wrong sort of flour so with its hunched shape, messy chocolate icing and thirty-two spiky candles sticking out at bizarre angles, it had ended up looking like a deformed hedgehog.

'This is *so* yummy!' Lauren had said, bravely eating a second piece.

She'd winked at Dee as she spoke, drawing her in, making her feel like a conspirator, a fellow grown-up. It was easy to see why Dad liked her, why anyone would like her. She was slim, pretty, lovely skin. Dee remembered noticing the skin, that first time. Very fresh, glowing, lightly tanned. Fake probably, she realised now. Like the rest of Lauren.

After the cake, Lauren produced some balloons from her handbag and they'd all played silly party games. Then, before she'd left, Lauren had given them each a little present, as if it was their birthday, not hers! Dee wasn't sure what the boys had got; there'd been so many gifts from Lauren over the years but Dee's first had been a silver bracelet with six tiny silver dolphins hanging from it.

'Are we going to see Lauren again?' Dee had asked later, when Dad came up to say goodnight.

'Would you like to?'

'Yeah!' she'd said, slipping the bracelet from her wrist and laying it gently on her bedside table.

After that they'd seen Lauren every weekend and, before long, she started coming round in the evenings, cooking their meals, washing their clothes or doing their ironing.

'Taking the strain off your dad a bit,' as she put it.

Dad had certainly seemed less strained. With Lauren around, he had time to play with them more, take them places again. He acted younger, too. Dressed younger in the clothes Lauren bought him from trendy, expensive shops. Lauren bought stuff for them as well, fussed over them, spoilt them, laughed and joked with them, so it wasn't only Dad who was besotted, back then – they all were. Lauren became so much of a fixture that Dee barely noticed when she stopped going home at night. It just seemed natural somehow that Lauren would stay, that she and Dad would eventually get married.

'As soon as my divorce comes through,' Lauren had said. 'Alan's been a right pain about it, which is a bit rich as it was him who wanted the divorce in the first place. Left me for a blonde bimbo barely out of school. But, hey, that's all past now. He did me a favour, I reckon,' she'd added, clutching Dad's arm.

Less than a year later, at the wedding, Lauren made out like it was her who'd left Alan.

'Because he didn't want kids,' she said. 'And I just love kids!'

No one questioned it. By that time they'd got used to Lauren's little fantasies. Had stopped trying to untangle fact from fiction. The way she'd tell you one thing, then give you a completely different version ten minutes later. It was just the way Lauren was; part of her bubbly over-the-top personality and it all seemed harmless enough. So harmless that they'd sort of overlooked the other weird stuff like the fact that Lauren didn't seem to have any family – certainly none who turned up to the wedding. Hardly any friends turned up either, apart from a few of her workmates.

'And aren't I just so lucky,' Lauren had told her workmates, drawing Dee and the boys to her in a massive group hug, 'to have the best ready-made family in the whole world!'

And Dee had believed her, of course, believed that Lauren loved them, cared about them. But she couldn't have done, could she? It was all words. Empty words and lies. Because if she'd loved them...

'Are you coming to badminton?'

Dee turned to see Sanjay standing right beside her, holding a racquet and a box of shuttlecocks.

'Oh, no, sorry. Completely forgot. I'm waiting for Scott but he hasn't turned up.'

'He's on his way, I think. He's been helping Mrs Mitchell move some books. So you won't be coming then? To badminton?'

'No, I'll leave it till next week, I think, when Hazel's back.'

Sanjay turned towards the sports complex, then turned round.

'So what you doing Friday then?'

'Friday?' said Dee, wishing she could manage something a little more intelligent than echoing Sanjay.

'Friday night. It's just that we're doing a gig. Only at the youth club. Nothing special. Just wondered if you fancied it.'

He wasn't asking her out. He was just checking whether she'd be around, hoping to make Abbie jealous, probably. Like Abbie said.

'I don't know,' was the best Dee could manage. 'Maybe.'

Hazel went straight to the classroom on Thursday morning. She couldn't face the common room. Couldn't face school at all really but Mum had insisted.

'I don't want you getting behind, messing up your exams,' Mum had said.

As if Hazel was supposed to concentrate! As if any of it mattered. But she'd come in anyway, not wanting to heap on any more stress at home. Especially not after the way her sister had reacted. Sarah had lost it, lost it completely at the hospital on Tuesday, when the doctor had explained the 'anomaly', when Sarah had had to face the truth. She'd been so bad, she hadn't even been able to drive home. Mum had driven! Mum had been amazing, totally amazing, telling them the facts, calmly, blandly almost.

'It's only a small lump,' she'd said. 'They think it's malignant but hopefully they've caught it early enough. It won't have spread.'

Malignant. The word had lodged in Hazel's head, as if the syllables, the letters themselves were cancerous, expanding, spreading their blackness, driving out all saner, more rational thoughts. She was vaguely aware that the classroom was filling up, that the teacher had arrived. She was supposed to tell him or hand in the note that Mum had written.

'It's probably best that they know,' Mum had said.

Hazel got up, put the note on Mr Jenson's desk, walked back and sat down again. She supposed everyone would find out, sooner or later.

'Do you have to?' Abbie snapped.

'What?'

'Blank me like that! I mean, what is it with you this term?'

'Nothing.'

'It's Tom, isn't it?'

'No.'

'Yes, it is!' said Abbie, raising her voice, attracting the attention of half the group. 'It's since I told you about Tom. Like you're jealous 'cos I'm not hanging around with you lot no more. It's not my fault if I've suddenly got a life. I mean, ignoring me in school's not gonna help, is it?'

Hazel shook her head, unable to speak, desperate for Abbie to stop. She couldn't be doing with any of this. She just wanted to be left alone but still Abbie droned on.

'Don't bother denying it. Just grow up and stop being so pathetic.'

Mr Jenson stood up, put the note he'd been reading back in the envelope.

'Give it a rest, Abbie,' he said, quietly.

'Why?' said Abbie, not even noticing Hazel's tears. 'She started it. Going all childish and sulky on me 'cos of...'

'Don't,' said Hazel. 'Don't say it. It's not Tom. It's got nothing to do with bloody Tom. It's my mum. She's got cancer.'

'O-my-god!' breathed Abbie.

Hazel stood up, feeling the sickness rising, feeling eyes watching her, hearing footsteps behind her as she headed for the door. She didn't get far. Out on the corridor a group of younger kids shrieked, giggled nervously as she leaned against the wall, vomiting.

'I'm sorry,' she heard Abbie say. 'Hazel, I'm so sorry.'

'Good,' said Mr Jenson. 'So now do something useful. You and Tasha get people off this corridor and keep them off. Joe, get the caretaker. Dee, see if you can get Hazel as far as the toilets or the medical room and I'll give her parents a ring. Get someone to come and pick her up.'

'No!' said Hazel. 'Don't do that. I'll be fine.'

The medical room was busy and after ten minutes or so Hazel announced she was feeling a bit better and was going to the library, where it was quiet.

'I'll come with you,' Dee said, 'if that's OK.'

The library was empty apart from the librarian who drifted off about ten o'clock. As soon as she'd gone Hazel pushed her books aside and looked intently at Dee.

'I know this is a bit personal,' said Hazel. 'An' you don't like talking about your family and stuff but, er, I mean, you don't live with your mum, do you? And I sort of wondered – whether your parents are divorced or what?'

'Mum died,' said Dee. 'Car accident. When I was seven.'

No point mentioning that she'd once had a step-mum. No point mentioning Lauren. No way did she want to go into all that.

'I'm sorry.'

'It's OK,' said Dee.

'I'm sorry,' said Hazel again. 'It's just that...'

'Hey,' said Dee, stretching out her hand, touching Hazel's arm.

She was going to say something cheery, optimistic, about how cancer wasn't the end of the world these days, about all the amazing new treatments, how loads of people made a full recovery but she didn't know. Didn't know how far it had got with Hazel's mum, didn't want to mutter some stupid platitude until she knew the facts.

'Tell me,' she said, instead. 'It might help. Just to talk to someone, yeah?'

'They're going to operate,' Hazel said. 'Next Monday. She goes in Sunday night. I mean, she doesn't have to have a mastectomy or anything. So that's good, isn't it? They're just gonna take the lump out, check that it hasn't spread, to the lymph nodes or anything. But what if it has? Mum says not to think like that. But I can't help it. How do you cope when...'

'You won't have to,' said Dee, speaking quietly, firmly, like she'd learnt to do with Scott. 'Your mum's right. Don't even think that way. They're operating early, aren't they? So the chances are, it won't have spread. You have to believe that.'

It sounded false somehow, hypocritical, lecturing Hazel on positive thinking. Hazel said it had helped but her unfinished question had haunted Dee throughout the day, was still with her, as she sat next to Hazel in

65

General Studies, supposedly watching a video about pollution.

'*How do you cope when . . .*'

How do you cope when you lose someone? The truth was that you didn't. Not deep down. But she could hardly tell Hazel that, could she? Oh, you learnt to function, to go on, to adapt and even the emptiness filled up in time but it left you weaker somehow, more vulnerable. Left you expecting the worst out of life, not the best. Not all the time, maybe, but sometimes. Like when Dad had that first accident. She'd flipped, totally flipped.

She fixed her eyes on the video but her mind was somewhere else. Back in Liverpool, about six months after Lauren and Dad got married. During the Easter hols when Dee and her brothers had been packed off to their grandparents so Dad and Lauren could do some decorating. Not *these* grandparents but her mum's parents, Nana and Pops, who lived in a village between Liverpool and Knowsley.

They used to see a lot of Nana and Pops till Lauren had a massive row with them and all contact stopped for a while. But that particular Easter holiday had been good, brilliant in fact until they got the phone call, from Lauren, at the end of the second week.

'Peter had a bit of an accident yesterday,' she'd told Pops. 'Nothing serious. Fell off the ladder when he was painting the kitchen ceiling. He'll be all right but he's a bit peaky so could you hang onto the kids for another couple of days?'

No chance. No chance at all. The minute Pops mentioned 'accident' the fear had struck like a million sharp needles plunging into every centimetre of Dee's body.

'I want to see him!' she'd screamed, setting both Scott and Kieran off crying. 'I want to go home. I want to see him. I want my dad!'

She'd cried all the way home in the car. Not expecting her dad to be there. That's what accidents meant. That people didn't come back. The relief that he *was* there had stopped her tears but only for a second until she took in the plaster cast on his left arm, the swelling round his left eye and the bruises on his cheek.

'You said it wasn't bad!' she'd accused, glaring at Lauren.

'We didn't want you getting all upset, like this,' Lauren had said, wiping away Dee's tears. 'That's why we wanted you to stay with Nana, till some of the bruising went down. And it will. In a day or two. It's not so very bad. Your dad'll be fine, if we both look after him, eh?'

Dee had nodded, feeling a bit weird, a bit disorientated. Not just because of her dad and the accident and everything. There was something else. Something she didn't totally grasp until she was getting ready for bed. It was the house. It hadn't only been decorated, it had changed completely.

'Minimalist,' Lauren had called it but to Dee it had just looked empty.

All the walls were painted white. Every single one! Mum's tapestry cushions, her vases, her ornaments had gone. The family photos, which had hung in the hall and up the stairs, had gone, along with all the albums off the bookshelves.

'It's all right,' Lauren had said. 'They're safe. I've put them in a box in the attic. We're going to have a couple of lovely modern paintings instead. You can help me choose. And wait till you see the new stuff we've got for your bedroom!'

The new stuff, as Lauren had hinted, was fantastic but the biggest shock had been Kieran's room.

'Wow!' he'd yelled, staring at the Liverpool FC curtains, rug and banner he'd been pestering about for ages.

He was so busy admiring the huge banner that covered the whole of one wall, that it took him a while to realise his bed was missing and in its place was a pine bunk.

'So you and Scott can share,' Lauren had explained.

'Why?' Kieran had asked. 'Why do I have to have him in my room?'

'Come and see,' Lauren had said, leading them to the smallest room at the back, the one that had belonged to Scott.

She threw open the door to reveal more white walls but ones with a border of little yellow ducklings, matching the ones on the curtains. From the ceiling colourful mobiles dangled and, in the corner was a cot.

'You're having a baby!' Dee had said.

'Not just yet, but we're hoping, aren't we, Peter?' Lauren had said, holding onto Dad's good arm.

Dee shook her head, trying to rid herself of the image of that room, the room that had stayed empty because Lauren never did get pregnant. She refused to go for tests. Hated doctors and hospitals, she said. Wouldn't even let Dad go when he started with his dizzy spells and stomach upsets, shortly after the decorating fall, which is what had caused the mega-row with Nana and Pops.

'You need to go and get yourself checked out, Peter,' Nana had said. 'You look terrible. It could be diabetes, blood pressure, anything. Or the fall could have damaged something, set off a reaction.'

'I'm fine,' Dad had said. 'It's nothing. Just work stress.'

'Doing too much, as usual,' Lauren had said. 'You know Peter! He'll be OK once he gives up some of the extra work, has a decent holiday.'

Nana had made the mistake of pushing it. Even contacted Gran and Granddad to tell them she was worried, which is when Lauren had really kicked off.

'It's nothing to do with you!' she'd yelled at Nana and Pops. 'Peter's married to me now, not your flaming daughter!'

The row had been terrible. Nana and Pops had stormed out. But it seemed, afterwards, as though Lauren might have been right. Under Lauren's instruction, Dad gave up on the book he was writing, on the evening classes he ran. He started to spend more time at home and, sure enough, he got better. He stopped being sick, stopped feeling dizzy, stopped falling over, being clumsy and bumping into things – at least for a time.

Dee shivered. She wasn't supposed to be thinking about any of this. She was supposed to be thinking about Hazel. Hazel's problem. No, not even that. She was supposed to be watching a video. Her eyes, she realised, were still fixed on the screen but the screen was blank. Someone was talking. The teacher. Standing close by.

'Well?' the teacher said.

Was he looking at her or Hazel? Had he just asked a question?

'Nuclear waste,' said Joe, swinging round on his chair.

'That's right,' said the teacher. 'Nice to know someone's been paying attention.'

Dee smiled gratefully at Joe but Hazel didn't react at all, as though she hadn't even realised what had been going on.

'It'll be OK,' Dee told Hazel, as they started packing up.

What else could she say? At least with Hazel's mum they were doing something. Unlike with Dad, where they'd left things, ignored them, refused to see, were incapable of seeing, what was happening, until it was all way out of control.

6

Abbie darted into the common room, picked up her jacket but didn't bother putting it on. It was too hot. Late afternoon on a Friday near the end of October and the sun was still blazing like it was high summer in the Sahara. Half term seemed to have come round really quickly and it was going to be brill, fantastically, wonderfully, amazingly mega-brill. Tom had got the whole week off and they were going to spend every possible minute of it together. Just the two of them, without Paige and Leo. He'd promised.

OK so she had homework to do, coursework to start, not to mention all the outstanding stuff her teachers had been whingeing on about. And the letter had probably arrived by now: the 'serious concerns' letter the school was sending home. But what the heck. Her parents could whine, moan, sulk but they couldn't stop her going out, could they? Tom was right. School was boring, school was for kids. If she got kicked out it would save all the hassle of trying to persuade her parents to let her quit, wouldn't it?

'You're quick off the mark,' Hazel said, coming in just as Abbie was heading out.

'Yeah well Tom's picking me up at seven so I've got to get ready.'

'OK but don't forget Wednesday night,' said Hazel.

Wednesday, Wednesday? What the heck was happening on Wednesday night?

'Hazel's *birthday*,' said Joe, who was hovering close to Hazel as usual.

'Duh! I know!' said Abbie. 'Wouldn't forget my best mate's birthday, would I?'

'And you're bringing Tom?' asked Hazel.

'Yeah, I've told him. It's all arranged. See ya then,' said Abbie, bouncing out.

Tom hadn't been exactly thrilled at the idea, when she'd mentioned it, but he'd come round. He'd only agreed to meet her friends, briefly, a couple of times during the past few weeks and he hadn't been too keen on any of them. Said they were boring. But then that first time Hazel had been sort of quiet, moody, not quite at her best – with the worry about her mum and everything. In fact, it had been shortly after the operation and Hazel had only been around for about ten minutes 'cos she was on her way to the hospital. In a complete panic 'cos they were due to get some results or something.

And the second time, when they'd bumped into the whole crowd accidentally in town, Tom had got in a strop about Sanjay, which was stupid, especially as Sanjay definitely seemed to have something going with Dee now. Though what sort of 'something', Abbie wasn't quite sure and didn't much care.

She couldn't really imagine what Sanjay saw in Dee at all. Tom had been totally right about her! She was so dull, always in the library, always working, unless she was fretting about her freaky brother or fussing over Hazel, asking about her mum all the time.

Funny that. Dee asked loads of questions about other people's families but said hardly anything about her own. Most of the time she was dead quiet; secretive almost. She'd been there six weeks and they barely knew anything about her! Pretty. Yeah, she was kind of pretty though she didn't exactly make the best of herself. Mid-length hair, tucked behind her ears most of the time, and she wore hardly any make-up.

Come to think of it, Dee and Sanjay were probably well-suited. Sanjay never bothered about getting his hair cut properly. He still let his mum snip away at it. How bad was that? She used to think Sanjay was dead cool, dead mature until she met Tom. Now all her old friends seemed childish. Oh, God, Wednesday night was going to be awful. Tom was gonna hate it.

But it couldn't be helped. No way could she miss Hazel's birthday.

'Happy Birthday to you,' Sarah and Hazel's parents sang, as Lucy banged out a discordant accompaniment with her spoon.

Hazel cut the cake that Sarah had brought and hastily mashed up a small piece in Lucy's dish to distract her from spoon banging. Mum wasn't feeling too bad now but she couldn't be doing with too much noise, too much fuss.

'Whoops,' Mum said, as Lucy promptly flicked yellow mush at Sarah. 'All over your new top!'

Dad frowned at the word 'new'.

'It's OK,' said Sarah. 'Two fifty from Oxfam.'

Charity rather than designer shop. Two pounds fifty rather than two hundred and fifty! Hazel tried not to look surprised. Sarah was really taking this economy drive seriously. The one she'd launched into when Mum went into hospital.

'Well I have to, don't I?' Sarah had said. 'Now we've got Lucy to think about.'

Lucy wasn't the only reason, though. The main reason, the one Sarah didn't want to talk about, was to take any extra worry away from Mum. Not that Mum had seemed unduly worried! She'd been totally positive before the operation, after the operation and during the agonising

75

wait for the results, which would tell them whether the cancer had spread. Utterly confident that it would all be a success. And, largely, it had been. The results had come back clear; the radiotherapy Mum was having was merely a backup, a precaution, the doctors had told them.

There would have to be regular check-ups, of course, and Mum was still a bit tired, run-down. She was supposed to be taking things easy for a while so Hazel hadn't wanted to bother with birthday celebrations at all but Mum had insisted on doing lunch for the family and Joe had organised a Chinese meal for the evening, bravely volunteering his house for a sleep-over.

'Go on,' Mum had urged, when Hazel had initially refused Joe's offer. 'It'll do you good to have a proper night out. You can't hang around here, checking up on me forever. I'm fine now, honest.'

Maybe Mum was right. It would be good to get out, try to relax a bit after all the stress and it was ages since they'd had a decent party. Ages since Abbie had joined them for anything other than lessons. Even then, Abbie had been sort of distant, distracted. She spent most of her time texting Tom, had barely asked about Mum and barely seemed to care how Hazel was feeling – unlike her other friends, who'd been brilliant.

'Some people feel awkward about illness, don't they?' Dee had said. 'Maybe Abbie's just not sure what to say.'

'And maybe she's just turning into a selfish cow,' Joe had said, more bluntly. 'I mean empathy's hardly her strong point at the best of times, is it?'

But then Joe was always way too harsh where Abbie was concerned, always going on about her being shallow and vain; ignoring all her good points.

'She uses you, Hazel,' he'd say, when he was feeling particularly brave. 'It's all one-sided with Abbie, self, self and more self.'

Well, he was wrong. It wasn't like that. Abbie was a good mate. The best. Fun to be around. The sort who'd always cheer you up just by being there. Until recently, of course. Since Tom came along.

'Are you going to open your presents or what?' Sarah was asking.

'Oh yeah, right!' said Hazel, picking up one of the parcels.

Maybe it would be better after tonight, after they'd had a chance to meet Tom properly. The couple of times she'd seen him, he'd seemed a bit sort of sneering, arrogant almost but, to be fair, she'd never really had a proper conversation with him or anything. And if Abbie liked him so much, he had to be OK, didn't he? So there was no reason why they shouldn't all get on, was there?

'Where are we going?' Abbie asked as Tom turned left out of her road instead of right.

'Back to the hotel,' said Tom. 'Paige is working till ten so we'll just have a drink, hang around till she's finished. Maybe drive down to a club in Lancaster, later.'

'Hang on,' said Abbie. 'It's Hazel's birthday.'

'So?'

'So we're supposed to be going.'

'You should have told me,' said Tom. 'I just love kiddy parties. Jelly and ice cream, yum!'

'It's not a kiddy party,' said Abbie. 'It's a meal at The Silver Lantern. And I did tell you. We talked about it. You promised you'd go!'

'No,' said Tom, half turning to smile at her. 'It's news to me.'

'Can't we go anyway?' pleaded Abbie. 'Just for an hour or so. Then meet up with Paige and Leo later, if you want.'

'It's just Paige,' said Tom. 'Leo's gone off on one of his jaunts. And we'd be in no state to meet up with Paige if we went to The Lantern first, would we? We'd be at A&E with food poisoning. It's a dump!'

'It's not,' said Abbie. 'It's got new owners. It's fantastic now. Mum and Dad went the other week. Please,' she added. 'It's important.'

'Fine,' said Tom, his smile disappearing as he swung the car round. 'I'll drop you at The Lantern, if that's what you want. If you'd rather be with your pathetic mates than with me. We were supposed to be spending the whole week together though, if you remember? That's why I took time off.'

Abbie could have pointed out that he'd broken his part of the deal already, that they'd seen Paige and Leo every single flaming day so far. But it was no use. Tom would only start having a go at her for being childish, for whining all the time, and no way was he going to change his mind about Hazel's party. She'd just have to go on her own. Make up some excuse for Tom.

'It's all right,' Tom was saying. 'I'm sure me and Paige'll find some way to entertain ourselves.'

He didn't mean it. He was just teasing, winding her up. She didn't have to worry about Paige. Tom and Paige were just friends. He'd told her that.

'She flirts with everyone,' he'd said. 'You don't have to make out like it's a big deal! It's you I love. You know that.'

But did she? Sure he told her he loved her almost every day. Told her she wasn't like any of his ex-girlfriends. Claimed she was special. That he'd known, from the minute he'd seen her in the café, they had a future together. She'd felt it too: that wild, crazy feeling that was still there every time he looked at her, smiled at her. Every time she thought about him. The knowledge, the certainty that Tom was all she'd ever wanted, that there simply wasn't a future without him.

So why spoil it? Why risk losing him just for a birthday meal that she probably wouldn't enjoy anyway. Couldn't enjoy without Tom. Hazel wouldn't miss her. Not with the whole crowd going. Twenty-five, Hazel had said, with at least a dozen of them staying over at Joe's.

Nothing would happen between Paige and Tom, of course, if she went to the party. That wasn't the point. The point was that Tom would be upset, hurt, disappointed. His face was already creasing into a sulk that could last for days. And she couldn't bear that, couldn't bear him being mad at her.

'I've changed my mind,' Abbie said, watching the scowl fade. 'I'll send Hazel a text. Tell her I'm not feeling well or summat.'

'Suppose that's goodbye to my wild night of passion with Paige then,' said Tom, as he turned the car once again. 'Only joking!' he added, winking at her. 'Go on. Text your friend.'

She opened her bag to take out her phone, saw Hazel's present, all neatly wrapped.

'Maybe we could drop her present round tomorrow, eh?' she said, knowing Tom wouldn't, knowing it would probably have to wait till Monday, till they were back at school.

Oh, well, it was no big deal. Hazel wouldn't mind. And, if she did, she'd get over it.

'Thanks,' Dee said, glancing at her watch as Sanjay dropped her home late on Thursday morning.

He turned the engine off, as if he expected her to invite him in but she couldn't do that. Not with Dad just back from his latest therapy session and no way of knowing what sort of state he'd be in.

'Bit of a bummer, Abbie not turning up last night,' said Sanjay. 'I mean,' he added, hastily, 'for Hazel. She looked right pissed off when she got that text.'

'Mmm,' said Dee, not taking the bait, not extending the conversation, wanting to get inside, find out how Dad had got on.

'I don't care about Abbie, you know,' said Sanjay, maybe misinterpreting her abruptness. 'Well, I do. But only as a friend.'

'I know,' said Dee. 'Sorry if I'm a bit off it. I'm just tired, that's all. Too much to drink, not enough sleep.'

'It's OK,' said Sanjay. 'See ya Saturday then?'

He sounded keen, like he always did. But was she still only a diversion to him, a way of getting over Abbie?

'Er, yeah,' she said. 'But if you just hang on a minute I'll go and grab that money I owe you.'

'It's OK. Saturday will do.'

'Oh, right, thanks,' said Dee as she got out of the car. 'I won't forget!'

When she got in, she found Dad and her grandparents in the kitchen. Dad was making tea. Not exactly the greatest challenge on earth but it was the first real task she'd seen him do on his own for ages.

'Can you do one for me?' she asked.

He nodded, carefully taking another mug down from the hooks.

'How did it go, then?' she said. 'The session?'

She'd addressed the question to her grandparents, not really expecting Dad to answer, but he did.

'Quite well,' he said, slowly. 'Quite well, I think.'

'She seems a bit different, this therapist,' Granddad said quietly to Dee. 'More sort of practical, looking forward instead of back. Setting targets as opposed to dredging up memories.'

'This is one of the targets,' Gran said. 'Doing little jobs. One or two each day, building up to walking to the local shops on his own before the next session.'

'Then, if I manage that,' said Dad, turning to face them, 'the following week I can try the supermarket.'

Was there a hint of the old dryness, the irony in his voice or was that too much to hope? More likely this was just the usual pattern. Optimism, signs of progress for the first few weeks of any new therapy, followed by relapse. The pattern was common enough. She'd looked up cases similar to Dad's on the internet. Sixteen years it had taken one poor bloke. Sixteen years and he still wasn't fully better, fully able to function properly.

'That's brill,' Dee said, pushing the depressing cases she'd read about to the back of her mind.

She picked up two mugs of tea and carried them to the table.

'So what about you?' Gran asked. 'Had a good time?'

'Yeah. Mainly. Couple of hitches like Hazel's best mate not turning up and me forgetting my purse. It was *so* embarrassing. Everyone throwing money on the table at the end of the meal and me scrabbling about in my bag for a purse that wasn't there! Luckily Sanjay had some spare.'

'Are you sure you forgot it?' said Gran, anxiously. 'I mean, did you leave your bag lying around? Could someone have taken the purse?'

'No, the bag was hooked over the back of my chair and I was wedged in against the wall. I reckon I must just have left it on the bed or in my school bag or something.'

'You'd better go and check,' said Gran.

Dee took her drink up to her room, checked the bed, her bag, the dressing table but the purse wasn't there. Could Gran have been right? Could someone have nicked it? The only people close enough had been Sanjay on her left and Sean on her right but neither of them would have touched her bag, would they? She didn't really know Sean that well. He seemed OK, honest, straightforward enough – but it was so easy to get people totally wrong.

She sat down on the edge of her bed, her mind having leapt from Sean to Lauren in an instant. Why? Why did every single bloody thing that happened remind her of Lauren? A missing purse, for heaven's sake! Why had that set her off? Lauren was a lot of things but she wasn't a thief. And, once thoughts of Lauren had got a grip, why were they so impossible to shake off? It wasn't as though thinking about it did any good. She'd been over it all a million times, trying to work out why and how it got so bad, looking for clues.

Clues that were blindingly obvious now, in retrospect, of course. Dad's mystery illnesses, Lauren's growing frustration that she couldn't get pregnant. But even that hadn't been clear, at the time. OK, so the 'baby room' gradually filled up with baby clothes and cuddly toys but there hadn't seemed anything terribly wrong with that. Traces of Dad's old life, his previous marriage to Mum, were gradually wiped out and family videos disappeared. But they were supposed to be in the boxes in the attic, weren't they? With all the framed photos and albums. Nobody bothered to check. Why should they? And, by the time they realised, it was too late. They were all in some landfill site somewhere.

Even the photos on the computer had been deleted. Accidentally, Lauren had said, when they'd asked. Probably one of the boys had done it by mistake!

Lauren didn't show any signs of depression. She was always upbeat. Always nice to them, always gushing on about how much she loved them. A little too keen to pack them off in the holidays on school trips or to various relatives and friends, but that was hardly cruelty, was it? Not exactly 'wicked stepmother' behaviour.

'Your dad and me like a bit of time on our own together, sometimes, don't we, Peter?' she'd say. 'It helps us to get things sorted out.'

What exactly needing sorting, Lauren never said. And Dad would simply nod, ever anxious to please, to keep Lauren happy. Because only Dad knew the secret, back then. Only Dad knew what might happen if Lauren wasn't happy.

Dee leaped up. Why hadn't he done something? Insisted they got help, saw a doctor? She knew the answers of course. Even realised they made a certain sort of sense. But it didn't help. She walked over to the chest of drawers, pulled one out, started searching amongst the socks and the underwear. Find the missing purse! Concentrate on that. Stop thinking about bloody Lauren!

7

The common room fell silent as Mrs Felby strode in at quarter to nine on the Monday morning after half term.

'Abbie?' Mrs Felby said, looking straight at Hazel. 'Has anybody seen her?'

'Don't think she's in yet,' said Hazel.

'What a surprise,' Mrs Felby snapped. 'Well, if she turns up, perhaps you could remind her that she was supposed to be outside my office at 8:30 with her work!'

Someone else could remind Abbie, Hazel thought, as Mrs Felby stormed out. *She* wasn't going to do it. She wasn't going to have anything to do with flaming Abbie. It wasn't just that Abbie hadn't turned up at the party or even that she hadn't bothered to send so much as a card; it was all the other stuff. Stuff she'd been trying to rationalise, excuse, defend! The way Abbie had hardly asked about Mum over the past few weeks or cared about what was going on. Abbie's parents had been round to see Mum again during half term, sent flowers when she was in hospital, asked if there was anything they could do to help but, from Abbie, barely a bloody word. Joe was right. Abbie was selfish and getting worse by the minute.

'You all right?'

'Yeah,' said Hazel, looking up at Dee. 'You? Did you find your purse?'

'No,' said Dee. 'I've just been looking in my locker, in case I left it here. Can't think what I could have done with it. I'm sure it'll turn up somewhere. Luckily my bank card wasn't in it so I was able to pay Sanjay and—'

The rest of the sentence was drowned out by the bell ringing and, as it stopped, the door opened and Abbie came in. People who'd already started to move froze, staring. Hazel's resolution to ignore her crumpled completely.

'Jeeez!' Hazel said. 'What's happened to your hair?'

'Had it cut,' said Abbie, doing an exaggerated twirl. 'Like it?'

'Er, yeah,' said Hazel. 'It's, er, very short. Nice, though. Bit of a shock, that's all.'

'I went with Paige,' said Abbie, 'to her hairdresser in Manchester. Mega-expensive but Tom paid. He says if you're gonna have a drastic cut, you've got to have the best. So what do you think?'

She was addressing her question to the whole room, not satisfied with just Hazel's approval. People dutifully muttered, nodded, smiled. It looked good. Anything would look good on Abbie. But better? Hazel wasn't sure. Long hair *was* Abbie, somehow.

'Mrs Felby wants to see you,' Joe said, amidst all the comments about the hair.

'Yeah, I know,' said Abbie, clutching onto Hazel's arm, holding her back until the others had gone out. 'Look, have you got any work? Anything I can copy and change a bit? Anything at all, just to keep her off my back? That English?'

There'd been a dozen or more pieces that Abbie hadn't done and Hazel had them all stored on her laptop but should she hand them over? If Mrs Felby found out, she'd be in dead trouble. And why should she bail Abbie out, anyway? It had been a real struggle keeping up with the work, keeping some sort of grip while Mum was ill. She'd managed – somehow she'd managed to get it all finished. She'd even got fairly decent grades. So why should she lend it to someone who was just bone idle?

'Oh, go on,' said Abbie. 'Pleeeeease!'

Hazel paused for a moment, then found herself nodding.

'Brill!' said Abbie, delving into her bag, producing Hazel's present and card. 'You're a real star.'

A tight knot had formed in Dee's stomach when she'd got the message from Mrs Mitchell to go to the unit at lunchtime. But she needn't have worried. Mrs Mitchell was pleased with Scott's progress. Thought he was doing so well that she wanted to put him back into more mainstream lessons.

It was always a bit awkward talking to Mrs Mitchell, knowing quite what to say, because they hadn't told the whole truth about Scott. They hadn't lied to the school, exactly, just kept it vague. There'd been some domestic problems, they'd said. Scott had been disturbed by them. It had made him ill. Talk about understatement! No wonder poor Mrs Mitchell was a bit bemused, a bit unsure how to proceed.

Dee looked at her watch. There wasn't really time to walk down and join the others in town so she headed for the library. Gran's house was all right but it was a bit crowded, a bit claustrophobic for the six of them, so it was easier to do homework at school, when she got the chance.

As she pushed open the library door, she paused, holding onto it to stop it squeaking shut. Abbie was sitting at one of the computers, with Sanjay next to her, his arm draped round the back of Abbie's chair. Although

89

Dee hadn't moved, had barely breathed, Sanjay turned, looked at her, got up and followed as she backed out.

'Hey, hang on,' he said, catching up as she hurried down the corridor towards the common room. 'I was just giving Abbie some work. The stuff I did for Music last year.'

'Sanjay!' said Dee. 'She can't copy that! She's already copied a whole load of stuff from Hazel. She'll get banned from exams completely if anyone finds out.'

'She's not gonna copy it,' said Sanjay. 'She's just gonna use it as a basis. Besides, there won't *be* any exams if she doesn't catch up a bit.'

'Yeah, well,' said Dee, turning into the common room. 'Suit yourself. It's none of my business, really.'

'Not mine either,' said Sanjay, sitting next to her. 'But I'm sort of worried about her, you know. She's just changed so much, since she's been with this Tom bloke.'

'Well, I didn't know her before but from what everyone's said . . .'

'It's not just the hair and work and stuff,' Sanjay interrupted. 'I mean, have you seen what she's eating?'

'Haven't see her eat anything much.'

'Exactly,' said Sanjay. 'A few grapes and a bit of chopped carrot, she had for lunch today. She's lost loads of weight. You must have noticed! Says she wants to get down to a size eight or even a six like that Paige person she keeps droning on about. I mean, that's tiny, innit? What size are you?'

'Twelve.'

'Yeah,' said Sanjay, looking at her, closely. 'That's what Abbie used to be, I think.'

'And she's taller than me,' said Dee.

'Yeah, so that's not even slightly overweight, is it? But Tom said she was getting a bit fat round the hips so off she goes on this stupid diet. I don't get it. If I'd said that she'd have kicked me in the balls!'

'Point is,' said Dee, 'you wouldn't have said it, would you? Or told her where and how to get her hair cut. 'Cos you're not a control freak, are you?'

'And you reckon Tom is?'

'Looks that way,' said Dee, her throat tightening as she spoke.

'So why does she put up with it?' said Sanjay. 'Why's she being so pathetic? It's just not like Abbie.'

Dee shook her head, the constriction in her throat making it difficult to speak.

'It's not pathetic,' she muttered. 'It's a sort of gradual thing. You get hooked on someone. Want to hold onto them. Want to please. To the point where you barely see what's happening to the relationship, to your life.'

She paused, partly because she didn't want to talk about it any more and partly because Sanjay was staring at her.

'Have you been involved with someone like that, or something?' he said.

'Me?' she said, a bit too hastily. 'No.'

'But you know something about it, something like it?'

'Sort of,' said Dee. 'Maybe.'

'So could you talk to her?'

'What?'

'Abbie! Just talk to her. Try to get her to see sense a bit. I mean, I can't, can I? She'll just say I'm jealous of Tom, won't she? And she won't listen to Hazel either these days.'

'Well, she's not going to listen to me, is she? She barely ever talks to me now, unless she wants something.'

'She might,' said Sanjay. 'Just give it a try, eh? If you get a chance.'

Was Sanjay a bit too interested in Abbie, a bit too keen for her to wise-up and dump Tom? So he could get back with her?

'I'm not still interested in Abbie, you know,' Sanjay said, as if reading Dee's thoughts. 'Not in that way. I think I was at first,' he added, 'when I first started seeing you. But I'm not now. Honest. Just don't want to see her totally screw up, that's all.'

Maybe Abbie wouldn't screw up. Maybe things would settle once the novelty of Tom started to wear off. Dee wasn't convinced but she was fairly sure there was nothing she could do about it. As predicted, Abbie barely spoke to her, barely looked at her that week, let alone gave her a chance to launch into a cosy little chat – until late on Friday afternoon. Dee was in the library and, as always on a Friday afternoon, she had it to herself until Abbie burst in, flinging a pile of folders and papers onto the desk. A copy of Abbie's timetable fluttered to the floor and Dee picked it up.

'I'm supposed to get that signed,' Abbie said, 'by the bloody librarian. All my free time I've got to spend in here, Mrs Felby says! Till I get the work finished. I mean, I've done some of it. But is it good enough? No! She wants another five pieces by Monday. How am I supposed to do that?' she added, glancing at the clock. 'There's only twenty minutes left.'

'You could do some over the weekend,' Dee tried. 'Surely you don't see Tom all the time?'

'Most of it, yeah,' said Abbie. 'When he's on shifts, I go up to the hotel, help out, so we can be together a bit more.'

She sat down, stretched her legs out, pushed the work away and sprawled her arms over the back of the chair.

'Well, she can stuff it,' Abbie announced. 'I'm not doing it. I'm quitting, like Tom says. Right now! I'm not coming back next week.'

Dee looked round. The librarian was at her desk, studiously ignoring Abbie's outburst.

'Are you sure that's a good idea?' Dee said.

'Best I've had today!'

'And it's what you really want? Not just what Tom says?'

'Oh, don't you start,' Abbie snapped. 'What is it with people? I'm happier than I've ever been – or at least I would be if people left me alone. But oh no! All everyone wants to do is spoil it!'

'I don't think that's what they're about,' said Dee. 'I think they're worried about you, that's all. I mean you haven't really known him that long, have you?'

'Long enough.'

'But what if you quit school, dump all your friends and then it doesn't work out?'

'Duh! You sound just like Mrs "don't put all your eggs in one basket" Felby, you do.'

'Bit of a cliché,' said Dee, smiling. 'But it's not bad advice.'

'It's fu . . . flaming awful advice,' said Abbie, glancing at the librarian. 'Things *are* gonna work out with Tom, but not if I'm stuck in every bloody night doing stupid homework. Tom wants me to get a full-time job at the hotel. Live with him.'

'You're doing it again,' Dee said.

'What?'

'Tom wants, Tom says.'

'So?'

There were a million answers, a million examples of where it could lead.

Lauren says we need another holiday. Lauren thinks we should get a bigger car. Lauren doesn't want us to see Nana and Pops again. Lauren reckons doctors are a waste of time.

But did she want to tell Abbie any of that? Would Abbie believe her anyway? Recognise the parallels with Tom?

'So,' said Dee, slowly, 'what happens when you don't agree with Tom about something?'

'Dunno,' said Abbie. 'We agree about most things.'

'But if you didn't,' Dee pressed on. 'If there was something you felt strongly about? What then?'

'How the hell should I know!' said Abbie, standing up, walking out, leaving her work on the table and the librarian shaking her head.

Abbie didn't bother waiting for the bell or the school bus. She set off walking, keen to get as far away from school as possible, then once the school was well out of sight, she phoned Tom asking him to pick her up. With a lift from Tom, there'd just be time to get home, grab some clothes for the weekend and get out again before her parents got home from work, and tried to stop her.

The new shoes Tom had bought her were hurting, pinching her toes, but she kept walking because it was so cold and it would take Tom at least twenty minutes to drive down. Typically, the weather had changed dramatically for the worse the day she'd had her hair cut and the wind was now blowing round her exposed neck, down her ears, making them burn and throb. The hair had caused a bit of a row. She hadn't really wanted to get it cut, but she hadn't told Dee that – mainly 'cos Tom had been right, of course. Short hair suited her. It was fine.

She pulled her jacket collar up. Anyway giving in to Tom about the hair was no big deal, was it? She could stand up to him when it mattered, when it counted. She'd refused the drugs, hadn't she? Even though Tom had said it would be all right, that it'd stop her being 'so bloody uptight' all the time. OK so she'd smoked a bit of dope. But everyone did that, didn't they? Well, everyone except her holier-than-thou school friends. And she'd tried the other stuff, a couple of times. But mainly she just let Tom and his friends get on with it. Even though she felt excluded, a bit pathetic, tired when the rest of them were just livening up.

That's why Tom did it. So he could work the long shifts and still 'have a life', as he put it. It wasn't like he was an addict or anything. It was just recreational and he could afford to buy the best, so it wasn't dangerous, he said. Maybe once she went to live and work at the hotel, he wouldn't do so much, would spend less time with Paige and Leo. But was she ready to take that step yet? Not if her parents had anything to do with it.

'No way,' Dad had yelled, when she'd hinted at it a couple of days back. 'No way are you giving up on school to go and work as a bloody chambermaid! And you're certainly not going to *live* up there.'

Mum had been a bit more restrained. Not saying anything until an hour or so later, when she'd knocked on the bedroom door. She'd hovered, while Abbie was getting ready, trying to be chatty, friendly, not getting round to what she really wanted to say until Abbie was nearly ready to leave.

'This business about living up at the hotel,' she'd said. 'I mean, you're up there such a lot already and you and Tom, well you're obviously...'

'Mum!' Abbie had warned.

'I know you're seventeen now, Abbie, but I just want to make sure you're being careful.'

God, parents were just so embarrassing! I mean, how would they like it if someone started prying into their sex lives? Advising them on contraception, like they were totally, totally stupid!

Abbie shoved her hands into her pockets to stop the ends of her fingers freezing off. Where the heck was

Tom? She was almost home when his car drew up quietly beside her.

'Sorry I'm late,' he said, as she slithered into the passenger seat. 'Got held up. Oh, you poor thing,' he added turning the heating up and rubbing her shoulder. 'You're freezing and your nose is all red, look!'

'Doesn't matter,' said Abbie, sliding her arms round his neck and kissing him.

The weather, school, friends, parents – none of it mattered. She relaxed her grip on Tom's neck, sat back in her seat and smiled at him.

'What?' he asked.

'Nothing,' she said, as he eased the car away from the kerb. 'You just make me happy, that's all.'

8

Hazel dumped a large cardboard box full of Christmas decorations on a chair in the common room, picked up a piece of silver tinsel from the top and draped it round her head, halo style.

'What do you think?' she asked her friends.

'Looks stupid,' said Abbie. 'God, you're such a kid, sometimes.'

'So?' said Hazel. 'Where's your festive spirit?'

'It'll surface in exactly three days when I get out of this dump for good.'

'You've definitely made up your mind then?' Dee asked.

'Yep,' said Abbie. 'I've done what everyone wanted, haven't I? Waited. Given it till Christmas. And it's still total crap. So I'm off. Out of here.'

Hazel shook her head and started sorting through the box. Sure, Abbie had compromised. After a whole load of grovelling from her parents, teachers and friends she'd agreed to carry on living at home, stay at school till the end of term. But she hadn't exactly given it much chance, had she? Skipping lessons, taking days off, dropping out of choir, giving up even any pretence of work. It'd probably be too late to catch up now even if she changed her mind, which she wouldn't.

'What you doing, anyway?' Abbie was asking.

'Mr Cotton's asked me and Dee to decorate the hall for the Year 7 party tonight.'

'Awww, how sweet.'

Hazel resisted the temptation to slap the slimy Tom-style smirk off her face.

'Want to help?' she asked.

'May as well,' said Abbie, yawning and stretching as she stood up. 'God, I'm knackered.'

'You'd have more energy if you ate summat,' said Hazel, as Abbie peered into the mirror, ruffling up her hair and baring her teeth.

'Tom reckons I should get my teeth professionally whitened,' she said. 'What do you think?'

'They look fine to me,' said Hazel, picking up the box of decorations and nudging open the door. 'But you'll probably do it anyway.'

'Mmm,' said Abbie vacantly. 'I'm just gonna text Tom. I'll be with you in a minute.'

Hazel managed to round up half a dozen others on the way to the hall, so it didn't really matter that Abbie didn't turn up till ten minutes before the end of lunch or that when she did, she perched on the edge of the stage, painting her nails. What mattered was the look on her face. The same look she'd had for weeks now. A look that was hard to define. A sort of cross between boredom and anxiety. An edginess, a nervousness that she'd never seen in Abbie before.

Was Abbie worried she was making a mistake? Was there still a chance to help her change her mind? Hazel handed over the paper snowflakes that she'd been pinning onto the hall curtains to Dee and went and sat down next to Abbie.

'You coming to the sixth form meal, tomorrow night?' she asked.

'What do you think?'

'I think Tom probably said he wouldn't be seen dead at a school party.'

'Wrong!' said Abbie. '*I* wouldn't be seen dead at a poxy school meal.'

Why, Hazel wondered, why was she doing this? Why was she even bothering? All she was going to get was a load of abuse as usual. They were hardly even mates any more, let alone best mates. How could that have happened? How could a friendship like theirs have crashed so completely in just one term? Was it all down to Tom or were they just growing apart? She'd changed herself, since Mum had been ill. She knew she had. It was like her whole life had been shaken up, all her priorities altered, but even so – her friends were still important, weren't they? She at least ought to try.

'You don't need to give up on the whole thing though,' Hazel suggested. 'You could talk to Mrs Felby again. Maybe drop a subject. Stay on till summer. See how you do in exams.'

Abbie stopped doing her nails. She put the brush back in the bottle, screwed the top on tight, put it in her bag and looked at Hazel intently. Was she thinking about it? Was she tempted?

'I mean,' said Hazel. 'We could all help out a bit. Help you catch up.'

'Hazel,' said Abbie, sweetly, as she slid down off the stage. 'How many times do I have to tell you? I'm happy. I know what I'm doing. I don't need your bloody help! So butt out.'

Dee stood in the porch, fumbling for her key, wishing someone had remembered to leave the light on. It was nearly eight o'clock. Very dark. No moon and only the faintest glimmer of stars. She'd stayed on after school to help with the Year 7 party, mainly because all her friends were helping but partly so she could keep an eye on Scott. Scott had been fine, though. He hadn't joined in the games but he'd talked to people and even volunteered to walk home with a couple of lads, while she stayed to clear up.

It had been weird listening to Joe and the others reminiscing about their own Year 7 party, comparing themselves with this new lot like they were a completely different species.

'Cheeky little sods,' Joe had said. 'That kid with the spiky hair told me to f-off when I took that bottle of cider off them. I mean we wouldn't have *dared* bring booze into school.'

'Or sworn at a sixth former,' Tasha had said. 'And did you see what some of those girls were wearing! We didn't wear tons of make-up at that age, did we? Not even Abbie!'

Hazel had walked off at the mention of Abbie's name and when Dee had caught up with her later, it was clear she'd been crying.

'I know,' Hazel had said. 'It's stupid. She's not worth it. And I'm not gonna bother any more. Why should I? She wasn't there for me, was she? All the time Mum was ill.'

Just as Dee found her key, the front door opened and Kieran appeared.

'Where you off to?' she asked.

'Out,' said Kieran. 'Just round to my mate's for a bit. Can't bear the excitement in there,' he added, nodding towards the lounge. 'They've been shopping today.

Bought a CD of yukky Christmas songs amongst other things.'

'Talking of which,' said Dee, 'have you done your Christmas shopping yet?'

'I told you, I haven't got no money. If you want me to buy presents, you'll have to get 'em and I'll pay you back.'

'Yeah, right,' said Dee, pushing past him and heading towards the lounge.

She paused in the doorway, putting her bag down, slipping off her jacket, staring at the tree in the corner that Dad, Scott and her grandparents were decorating with a garish assortment of baubles, woolly hand-knitted snowmen and the set of lights that had graced Gran's tree for as long as Dee could remember. It looked great! Mercifully different to the perfectly symmetrical 'themed' trees that Lauren used to insist on. And the best thing, the very best thing was seeing Dad and Scott so involved. Laughing, Dad was actually laughing. But Gran was looking serious, worried, as she turned and saw Dee.

'Are you hungry?' said Gran, walking towards her. 'I've left you a bit of lasagne in the oven.'

'I've been nibbling all night,' said Dee. 'But lasagne sounds good. It's OK, I'll get it myself.'

Gran followed her into the kitchen, hovering while Dee took out the lasagne.

'You know we went shopping today?' Gran said, sitting opposite Dee as she started to eat.

Dee swallowed hard, fearing the lasagne might catch in her throat. Had Dad had one of his panic attacks? Was that what Gran was building up to? Was the progress not as good as it seemed? Had it been a mistake for him to come off some of the anti-depressants?

'Well,' Gran went on. 'I had some money that I keep in a tin on my dressing table. You know what I'm like. I put in anything I've got left each week. It soon mounts up.'

Dee stopped eating, looked at Gran.

'And?' Dee said.

'After buying the boys' presents last week,' said Gran. 'I had just over two hundred left. I know because I counted it. But, this morning, when I came to get it out, there was only a hundred and fifty. And I wondered...'

'If I'd taken it?' said Dee.

'Good heavens, no!' said Gran. 'What I was going to say was I wondered whether you ever found your purse?'

'No,' said Dee, thoughtfully. 'No, I didn't.'

'I'm sorry,' said Gran. 'I didn't mean to upset you. Maybe it's just coincidence. Maybe I just miscounted. Can't really be anything else, can it?' she added, as if asking for reassurance. 'And don't say anything, will you? To your granddad or anyone?'

'Gran,' Scott said from the doorway. 'The tree lights have just gone out. Granddad wants to know where the spare bulbs are.'

Dee waited until they were all safely back in the lounge, put her lasagne back in the bottom of the oven and went upstairs to Kieran's room.

Tom led Abbie through the busy hotel kitchen, out the back, across the courtyard to the two-storey, modern blocks where some of the staff lived.

'What we doing?' Abbie asked.

'I told you,' said Tom. 'It's a surprise. Now close your eyes.'

Abbie dutifully closed her eyes, letting Tom guide her forward. She heard the click of a couple of doors and, when she was allowed to open her eyes again, found herself standing in a small room with a single bed pushed against the yellow-painted wall, the rest of the space taken up with a fitted wardrobe, a couple of shelves and a small table with two chairs. There were no books, clothes or other personal items. No bedding or towels. No sign that anyone lived here.

'Well?' said Tom. 'Do you like it?'

'Yeah, it's OK, why?'

'It's yours. I thought it might make your parents a bit

happier if you had a room of your own. Makes it seem more sort of respectable, doesn't it?' he said. 'Although I don't suppose you'll be spending much time here. My room's a lot, lot nicer,' he added, putting his arms round her, drawing her close.

'What?' he said, as Abbie pulled away and sat down on the edge of the bed. 'I thought you'd be pleased.'

Abbie tried to smile. She wanted to be pleased. She *was* pleased, in a way. And it was just so like Tom to be thoughtful.

'Hey!' he said, sitting beside her. 'Tell me. Tell me what's wrong.'

'I don't know,' said Abbie. 'I mean, I don't think this is gonna help. I had another row with them tonight before I came out and Mum was like crying all the time and Dad starts yellin' that he won't have no more to do with me if I go ahead with all this and...'

'They don't mean it though, do they? It's just emotional blackmail. What parents do best! My dad's always threatening to kick me out over something or other but he never does. And your mum'll come round.'

'Maybe,' said Abbie. 'But it's like I can't even talk to 'em any more. All we do is scream at each other.'

'So that's one of the reasons you're moving out, isn't it? 'Cos they're not ever going to let you grow up, are they?'

'Yeah, I guess, but...'

She stopped. Tom was glancing at his watch, looking bored already. He hated tears, problems, scenes. Life's too short, he usually said, to waste it worrying and whingeing. His phone bleeped.

'Bloody hell,' he said. 'It's Dad saying we were both due on shift ten minutes ago.'

'When I start working here proper,' said Abbie, as they walked back across the courtyard, 'I will get paid, won't I?'

'You're already being paid,' said Tom.

'Oh. Nobody said. Do I have to pick my wages up from the office or something?'

'No. I've got Dad to pay them straight into my account.'

'Er, your account?'

'Well, I'm going to change it to a joint account when I get a chance. Besides, I give you everything you want, don't I? Don't need any money at the moment, do you?'

'Not really,' said Abbie. 'I've still got my allowance but I sort of wanted to buy Mum and Dad something a bit special for Christmas. Show there's no hard feelings and all that. Try and make up to them a bit.'

'No probs,' said Tom. 'We'll go tomorrow, eh? Get you something nice for the staff party as well. Make a day of it. Have lunch out.'

'I can't. We don't break up for another two days.'

Tom laughed, hugging her as they walked into the hotel.

'Don't be daft!' he said. 'You're leaving! What difference will it make?'

Dee listened, waiting for the sound of Kieran's footsteps on the stairs, before pushing open her bedroom door.

'In here,' she said, as he tried to sidle past.

'What?' he said. 'Can't it wait till tomorrow? I'm knackered.'

'No,' said Dee, shoving him inside, picking up her purse off the bed and holding it in front of him, 'it can't!'

'Told you you'd find it eventually, didn't I?'

'You didn't tell me I'd find it in your room though, did you?'

'Maybe Scott picked it up, dumped it there and forgot to tell you. You know how ditzy he is.'

'It was under your bloody mattress, Kieran. And it was empty! So leave Scott out of this.'

'Well, you shouldn't have been in my room, should you?' said Kieran.

'You mean like you shouldn't have been in Gran's?'

'I 'aven't taken nothing,' said Kieran. 'I don't know how your purse got there. I didn't take your money and I didn't take Gran's neither.'

'Who said anything about Gran losing money?' said Dee. 'She hasn't told anyone else...yet. Not even Granddad.'

Kieran turned his flushed face away from her.

'It weren't me,' he muttered.

'It never bloody is, is it?' said Dee. 'Well, I've had it, Kieran. I'm sick of covering up for you. I'm sick of your lies. Stealing money from me, from Gran! It doesn't get much lower than that, does it? What's so important, Kieran, that you have to steal to buy it?'

'So what yer gonna do?' he said, ignoring her last question, turning to look at her, chin thrust forward, his face twisted into defiant challenge. 'Tell Dad? Tell Gran? Give her something else to worry about? You won't do anything, Dee. 'Cos you can't!'

He pushed her shoulder to nudge her out of his way. Not hard but enough to make her lose her balance, to stumble against the edge of the bed, to cry out as her shin cracked against the wood. She recovered in time to see Kieran's path blocked by another figure, a smaller figure. Scott. How much had he heard? How much had he seen? Had he seen the push, the fall?

His scream told her the answer.

A joint account, Tom had said. That must mean something, Abbie thought, as she wiped the tables in the residents' dining room. It must mean he was serious about her, that the things he said, the long-term plans, were for real.

She was working alone. Tom and Paige were supposed to be helping but they'd disappeared ages ago to pick up Leo from the station. Abbie wasn't quite sure what Leo did on his away-days, his jaunts, as Tom called them. Busking, allegedly! Pre-Christmas was always good, Leo reckoned, with everybody feeling festive and/or pissed.

She didn't know what time Leo was due back but Tom and Paige had been gone a couple of hours, at least. So maybe they'd stopped off for a drink somewhere, gone on to a club even. She'd texted Tom a couple of times but he hadn't replied. So what was she supposed to do, Abbie wondered, as she finished polishing the last table. He hadn't left her the key to his room, her new room wasn't quite ready yet and she didn't fancy going home. Not the way things were with Mum and Dad right now.

She could go and hang around in the bar. It stayed open all night. Or try and find a spare key for Tom's room. But she couldn't really be bothered. She was far too tired so she turned out all but one of the lights in the dining room and settled down on a window seat, peering out of the window that overlooked the staff car park, waiting for Tom's car to appear, until her eyes started to close.

She was woken by cold hands, touching her shoulders and the sound of Tom's voice.

'Oh, babes, sorry! I thought I'd be back ages ago but Leo's train was late.'

'Couldn't you phone?' Abbie murmured sleepily, as Tom's warm, whisky-tainted breath passed close to her face.

She pulled herself up.

'You haven't driven like that, have you?' she said, his eyes telling her that something more than alcohol had been involved.

She bit her lip, knowing how it had sounded, why it had set Leo and Paige off laughing.

'Couldn't you phone?' Tom mocked. 'You haven't driven like that, have you? Oh, Tom, you are *such* a naughty boy!' he added, slapping his wrist, prompting Paige to shriek even louder.

'She'll make you such a lovely wife, Tom,' Paige stage-whispered, when she'd finished shrieking.

Then Leo joined in. On and on they went; voices loud, tone light, words cruel until Abbie finally stood up.

'Oh, lighten up, can't you?' said Tom. 'We're only joking. What are you doing?' he added as Abbie got her mobile out.

'Phoning a taxi. I'm going home.'

'No you're not,' said Tom, snatching the phone off her. 'You'll go home when I say so.'

112

9

'Doesn't look like Abbie's turning up again today, does it?' said Sanjay, as they walked towards the church on the last morning of term.

There wasn't, Dee thought, much point any of them turning up really. Boring service for the whole school, an hour or so taking down Christmas decorations, early lunch and finish at two. But she'd sort of thought that Abbie would at least come and say goodbye. Not to her particularly, but to Hazel, Joe, Sean, Tasha and the rest. The people she'd grown up with.

They sat in the back pews, watching the rest of the school file in. Scott, with his head down, didn't notice her but Kieran paused and winked. It was weird. Almost like he was glad their bust-up had happened, pleased that Scott's freak-out had brought everyone rushing upstairs. He'd sat, telling their grandparents everything, or at least his version of everything, looking relaxed, relieved, as though negative attention was better than no attention at all.

The following day, Granddad had drawn up a plan with Kieran, a way to pay back the money out of his allowance, a new set of rules about where he could go and when. Whether it would work was a different matter. She'd seen Kieran full of good intentions before. But at least it wasn't her problem any more. Or at least she wasn't on her own with it.

Shuffling alerted her to the fact that the vicar had arrived, everyone was standing, opening their carol sheets. The service, mercifully, wasn't quite as dull as Dee expected. The vicar was quite young, funny and singing carols sort of revived everyone so they arrived back at the common room, totally hyper, singing *Jingle Bells*, behaving more like Year 7s than sixth form, until they heard Tasha squeal.

'Bloody hell, Abbie! What's happened to you?'

Dee pushed her way into the common room. What was it this time? Had Abbie gone blonde? Had a boob job or a face-lift? Got her nose remodelled to suit Tom's tastes? Dee heard Abbie before she actually saw her.

'Well me and Tom had a bit of a row the other night.'

There were gasps, murmurs from the audience; then Dee saw why. The side of Abbie's face, near her right eye, was bruised, swollen, the dark purple streaked with yellow. Dee leant against a chair, feeling suddenly sick. How could Abbie be so casual about it? Showing it off, like it was some sort of trophy instead of a serious assault!

'Anyway,' she was saying. 'He was like totally, totally sorry.'

As if that made it OK! Dee glanced at Sanjay, whose fists were clenched and she knew that if Tom had been in the room Sanjay would have gone for him.

'So he took me down to Manchester shopping,' Abbie was saying, drawing Dee back in. 'And we went to this like mega-expensive shop. It was dead small but with like mirrors everywhere and clothes to die for. No actual prices on anything, so I'm sorta really worried but Tom says to just pick anything I want.'

What, Dee wondered, as the sickness welled up from her stomach into her throat, was the going rate for a black eye? Two hundred? Two thousand?

'An' I try this fantastic dress on, right?' Abbie went on. 'But then I can't get out of the flaming changing room, can I? The door's jammed. I mean, expensive place like that and they don't even have decent doors on the changing room. So I think it's just me doing something wrong, so I give it a shove and it bursts open and I go with it flying across the shop, smack into the side of a clothes rail, with such a bang I think my eye's gonna pop right out!'

Dee sank down onto a chair. Not an assault. The black eye had nothing to do with Tom, with the row. It had happened later, in the shop. It was an accident.

'I must have actually passed out,' said Abbie, beaming, revelling in the attention. ''Cos next thing I know, I'm sitting on a chair, with Tom bathing my head. There's water dripping all down the dress, which is torn, and I'm like just soooo embarrassed. But as soon as Tom sees I'm OK, he gets really mad, telling 'em he'll sue for having the dodgy door and the clothes rail in the way.'

'What a bloody hero,' Dee heard Sanjay mutter.

'So 'course the owner's in a right flap, begging him not to sue and, in the end, we walk out of there with half a dozen bags of stuff, for free!'

Abbie carried on, giving a detailed description of the clothes to anyone who was interested. Describing every hemline, every fastener, every stitch.

'Fascinating as this is,' Hazel whispered to Dee, 'I'm gonna go and take the decorations down in the hall. Want to come?'

Dee nodded, rubbing her arms to keep warm as she followed Hazel, Sanjay and Joe.

'Blimey,' said Sanjay, as they went into the hall. 'I thought for a minute, back there, that Tom had hit her!'

'I think we were supposed to,' said Joe. 'That's our Abbie. Ever the bloody drama queen!'

'And you reckon the story was true?' said Sanjay, setting Dee off shivering again. 'You don't reckon she might have been covering up for him or anything?'

'Nah!' said Joe. 'Even Abbie's not that stupid, is she? If Tom had hit her, she'd have done summat about it, wouldn't she?'

''Spect so,' said Sanjay. 'What do you reckon, Hazel?'

'I don't know and I don't really care.'

'Me neither,' said Sanjay. 'But there was too much detail for it to be lies. I mean you wouldn't make up a complicated story like that just as a cover-up, would you?'

Oh, but you would. Dee tried to breathe deeply as she ripped down streamers from the edge of the stage. How many times had she heard stories like that?

'One minute I'm painting the kitchen ceiling and the next thing I know, I'm lying on the kitchen floor with my arm twisted underneath and the ladder on top of me.'

'I thought I'd pop in for a quick drink after work but I never got the drink, did I? Because this huge bloke with a dragon tattooed up his arm staggers out and smacks right into me.'

'I don't know how it happened, really. The traffic rushing past made me feel a bit dizzy I guess and I slipped off the kerb in front of a bike. Lucky it wasn't a lorry really.'

Only there never were any dizzy spells or a bike or a dragon tattoo or a huge bloke coming out of a mythical pub. Dee felt a sharp pain in her thumb and looked down to see a drop of blood oozing from where she'd pressed a drawing pin into the flesh. She pulled the pin out, quickly, sharply. Just because she'd heard stories, excuses, like that before didn't mean it was happening now. Abbie was probably telling the truth.

'Right, I'm off now,' said Abbie from the hall doorway. 'No point hanging around. Only came in to collect the rest of my stuff.'

Everyone turned to look at her but no one moved, so Abbie put down her bag and came towards them. She kissed Joe and Sanjay before wrapping her arms round Hazel.

'I'll miss you,' Abbie said, as Hazel's shoulders tensed. 'I mean it,' she added, pulling away. 'And I'll come round to see you over Christmas, eh? Catch up with Sarah and your mum and stuff. I mean, your mum's definitely OK now, right?'

Hazel nodded but said nothing.

'OK,' said Abbie, running her finger down the side of her swollen face. 'See ya.'

'I'll walk with you,' said Dee, on impulse. 'I need the loo.'

It was stupid. Stupid to interfere. But she had to try. She had to be sure. Abbie glanced at her, quizzically, as they passed the girls' toilets but didn't say anything until they got outside.

'Everything OK?' Abbie asked.

'Er, yeah, fine,' said Dee. 'You looking forward to all this then? New full-time job and everything?'

'You bet!'

'And everything's all right with Tom now?'

''Course,' she said, as if anxious to get away.

'Only you said about the row.'

'So?' said Abbie. 'Everyone has rows, don't they? Bet Sanjay pisses you off sometimes.'

'Not really.'

'Maybe you're a bit more patient than me,' said Abbie, suddenly smiling. 'He used to piss me off all the bloody time! At least Tom notices I'm around!'

'Abbie,' Dee said, as Abbie started to move.

'Go on,' said Abbie, turning back, moving in close. 'Say what you wanna say. There's obviously something bugging you.'

'OK,' said Dee. 'It's none of my business but I'm going to say it anyway. That stuff about the accident. It was definitely true, was it?'

'Duh!' said Abbie, pointing at her bruise. 'How do you think I got this? Think I painted it on for a bit of attention or summat?'

'No,' said Dee, feeling her courage ebbing away. 'It's just that some people thought that Tom...'

119

'Tom?' squealed Abbie, with an exaggerated laugh. 'As if!'

Was there a slight flicker of the eyes, a slight change of colour? Or was it imagination?

'It can happen,' said Dee. 'It gets out of hand. It . . .'

She stopped as her heart started to thud hard against her chest and her throat tightened making it impossible to breathe let alone speak.

'Hey!' said Abbie, putting down her bag, and steering Dee towards a bench as she began to cry. 'What's with all this?'

Dee still couldn't speak. The sobs were so deep, so intense now they were pulling across her chest like they were wrenching her ribs apart. And all the time she was aware of Abbie sitting there just staring at her, Abbie's voice gradually breaking through.

'Dee, what is it? What's wrong? You've gone white, totally white. Do you want me to get someone?'

'No,' Dee managed, eventually. 'I'm all right – I'm sorry.'

'It's OK,' said Abbie. 'But this isn't really about Tom'n'me, is it?'

'Sort of. Maybe. Thing is,' said Dee, the words gushing out between sobs before she could stop them. 'At the start, it's so easy to tell yourself it was an accident. The ladder toppled, no one pushed it. Or, if they did, they didn't mean to. And when they threw the

120

iron at you, they were aiming to miss, weren't they? Besides, they were really sorry. They were tense, stressed. It was a one-off, it wasn't going to happen again.'

'Dee,' said Abbie, quietly. 'What are we talking about here?'

Stop. This was the time to stop. Get up, walk away. While it was all still vague, general. But Dee couldn't. It was as though someone else had taken over. Some other Dee. And she couldn't stop her, couldn't shut her up.

'Lauren,' she said, 'my step-mother. Years it went on. Not constantly, not all the time. That was part of the problem. She'd be great in between, when things were going well. And, even when they weren't, she'd be fine on the surface, fine with other people, fine with us. It was Dad who was the target. Always when they were on their own. Like it was planned! Deliberate. Slapping him, punching him, kicking him or later, when it got really bad...'

'Bloody hell,' said Abbie. 'You hear about blokes beating up women but not the other way round!'

'Not so much, no,' said Dee, 'partly 'cos men are even less likely to talk about it, to get help. They feel sort of embarrassed, I guess.'

Dee bit her lip, trying to stop herself from going on but it didn't work. Memories of her dad's increasingly serious injuries pushed their way into her mind. The broken ribs, the scald on his arm when he'd allegedly dropped a pan of boiling water. And they'd accepted it all. They'd never once suspected. Not even when Dad started to withdraw into himself, becoming edgy, nervous, fearful, and angry. Angry with Gran and Granddad when they suggested, once again, that he see a doctor.

'People go on about stranger danger, don't they?' Dee said, her own anger bursting out. 'But it's not strangers who are the problem most of the time. It's people you're close to. People you love. Lauren even put glass in Dad's food. Can you believe that? Ground up bits of glass and put it in his food! He didn't realise, at first, what was causing the stomach upsets. And when he did, he never told anyone, never said anything. Just let it all go on and on and on.'

'Why?' Abbie breathed. 'OK so he might not want to tell anyone, get help or anything but why not just leave her?'

'It's not that easy, is it? If you love someone! I mean, would you walk out on Tom?'

'Yeah,' said Abbie, without hesitation, 'if he did stuff like that. Yeah, I would.'

'I don't know why Dad found it so hard,' said Dee. 'Not really. Partly 'cos of us, I think. 'Cos we were all so besotted with her. All thought she was so bloody great. She'd sort of filled the gap, after Mum died, you know? Made us happy again...happier, anyway.'

Abbie was staring, blankly, as if she didn't know, couldn't begin to imagine.

'And Dad thought she'd change, I guess,' Dee went on. 'That if he loved her enough, if he tried to make sure everything was all right, if they managed to have the baby she wanted, she'd be OK. I think he sort of felt sorry for her too. I mean, Lauren had all sorts of issues, apart from the infertility thing. Stuff Dad knew about but we didn't.'

'Like what?'

'Pretty sick, really gross stuff. She'd been abused as a kid. Trust me, you don't want to know the details. Besides, there was no telling, with Lauren, what was true and what wasn't. It could all have been a pack of lies, I suppose. But I don't think so. Anyway the point is, she was totally psychotic, totally screwed-up. Split-personality almost. And nothing Dad did could have made it right. No amount of love, no amount of babies would have made any difference. There would always have been something else. Something else she'd want, something wrong, something she'd blame Dad for. Only he didn't realise that. Not till it was all way out of control.'

Dee shook her head trying to make it all go away but it wouldn't. It just kept spilling out.

'It was *her* that couldn't have a kid. She knew that. But she couldn't accept it. So she blamed Dad.'

'Even though it was obvious he *could* have kids?'

'It's not logical,' said Dee. 'It's not rational. It's an illness. Like these people who cut themselves to allegedly stop their pain. Only Lauren didn't cut *herself*, did she? She...'

Dee leaned forward, retching.

'But your dad did get out of it, didn't he?' said Abbie. 'In the end? I mean, this Lauren, she's not around now?'

'No,' said Dee. 'She's not around now. But Dad didn't exactly get out of it. He was forced out. By what happened. By what happened to Scott. He...'

'You don't have to,' said Abbie. 'You don't have to tell me any more. Not if you don't want to.'

But it was too late. The words were still tumbling out. It was crazy. Telling Abbie, of all people! Telling her everything. Every last, horrendous detail of what had happened that New Year's Day, two years ago. When Dee had finished, Abbie sat, totally silent, her hands squeezing Dee's, which were white, freezing.

'Oh God,' Dee said. 'What have I done? I shouldn't have said any of that! I shouldn't have told you. You won't tell anyone? Please, promise me you won't tell anyone? It's important. Scott, Dad, they've both been getting better, tons better, since we've been here. But if it got out!'

'It won't,' said Abbie, firmly. 'Not from me. But . . . '

'What?'

'I can see why you got so freaked,' Abbie said, touching her bruised face. 'About this. But Tom didn't do it. He's nothing like your stepmum, Dee! He's a bit spoilt and he likes his own way, I grant you, but there's nothing dodgy about him. He's not violent and he wouldn't ever, ever hurt me. Not like that.'

Dee nodded. She'd been crazy even to think it. The chances that she'd ever come across anyone like Lauren again were tiny. Tom might be a control freak but then so were loads of people. It didn't mean they were psychotic or violent.

'Tom's OK,' Abbie was saying. 'He's more than OK. He's the best thing that's ever happened to me and I get so pissed off with people being negative about him all the time when they don't even know him proper.'

'I think it's *because* we've never really got to know him.'

'Yeah, well,' said Abbie, shrugging. 'He's a bit funny like that. Likes to stick to his own little clique of friends. And I don't mind. I'm getting used to 'em now. Even Paige! Speaking of which,' she added, glancing at her watch, 'I'm supposed to be meeting them down town in a bit. Look, will you be OK?'

'Yeah,' said Dee, as Abbie stood up, picked up her bag. 'I'll be fine . . . and good luck with everything.'

'You too,' said Abbie. 'Have a good Christmas, eh? Hey, look it's snowing.'

'More like sleet,' said Dee, shivering.

'Either way, you better go in before you freeze to death.'

Dee was already frozen, her muscles tight, aching. She went back into school, headed straight for the loos where she ran some hot water to warm up her hands. She dipped her hands into the sink, left them there, feeling the warmth filter through as she stared in the mirror, the same questions throbbing over and over in her head.

Why had she done that? How could she have been so stupid? Why hadn't she stopped herself? If Abbie told someone, just one other person, the story could spread. The thought of everyone knowing about it, talking about it, made her feel sick again. It was easy, in a way, to understand why Dad kept quiet all those years. Hiding it away, pretending it wasn't happening. Letting it gnaw away at his confidence, his self-esteem, until he'd really started to believe it was all his fault!

The sound of a loo flushing startled her. She'd thought she was alone. A second later one of the doors was pushed open and Hazel appeared.

'Hey!' said Hazel. 'Wondered where you'd got to. You OK?'

'Er, yeah,' said Dee, pulling out the plug and shaking her hands. 'I've been talking to Abbie.'

She paused for a moment.

'You and Abbie used to be dead close, didn't you? So you must have told each other stuff. I mean, if you told her something special, something personal, would she keep it to herself?'

'She'd try,' said Hazel. 'Abbie's not out and out nasty or anything. Wouldn't blab deliberately but, well, you know what she's like!'

'Meaning?'

'The mouth!' said Hazel. 'She doesn't think sometimes, does she? Just blurts stuff out. But probably not if it was summat dead important. Why? What's wrong? You look terrible!'

'No. I'm fine. It's nothing really,' said Dee. 'We just got talking, er, about Sanjay. And I told her something I wouldn't really want getting back to him.'

'Oh,' said Hazel. 'No. Should be all right. Yeah, I expect it'll be fine. Not least 'cos Abbie couldn't give a toss about Sanjay or any of us anymore. Don't expect we'll even be seeing her again, will we?'

10

Hazel sat at the kitchen table chopping cucumber into what she hoped were neat little cubes, mixing them into the salad, trying not to retch at the sight, the thought of food. The salad wasn't too bad but, over at the work surface, Dad was carving pale pink beef and opposite her Gary was spooning out great dollops of custard for the trifle with Lucy balanced precariously on his knee, gibbering, shrieking, making Hazel's head throb. It was her own stupid fault. She'd had far too much to drink last night at Tasha's party. Well, by her standards anyway. She wasn't good with alcohol. Usually managed to make a glass of lager shandy last all night!

'Oh, come on,' Joe had said, half a dozen times during the evening. 'Have another drink. If you can't enjoy yourself on New Year's Eve, when can you?'

Had he done it deliberately? Hoping she wouldn't resist when midnight came, when he made sure he was right beside her. If so, it had worked. She'd kissed him, danced with him till turned three when her taxi came, agreed to go out with him! She could change her mind, of course, but did she want to? Joe was fun, quite good looking if you ignored the silly moustache and she liked him, felt totally at ease with him. But was that enough? There was none of the raging passion that Abbie seemed to feel for Tom. And would she lose Joe as a friend if things didn't work out? Was it worth the risk? She'd have to decide pretty soon. She'd be seeing him again in a few hours. His family were coming over, as they always did for the New Year's Day party.

'We'll keep it small this year,' Mum had said but small had somehow escalated to over fifty people, so she, Sarah and Gary had been roped in to help with the preparations. As Hazel finished the cucumber and moved on to the spring onions, her phone beeped. She snatched it up, expecting it to be Joe but it wasn't.

'Surprise, surprise,' she said, slamming it down again. 'Text from Abbie to say she's not coming. She's working again. I haven't seen her once over the holiday. She didn't send any of us so much as a card or anything. Too busy, I guess!'

Dad and Gary mumbled sympathetically but neither seemed interested. They'd had their own little celebration last night. Nothing terribly wild, by the sound of it, but poor Dad had been up since half past five as usual for the milking. Hazel picked up the finished salad and carried it through to the dining room where Mum and Sarah were setting up, doing all the artistic bits. They stopped talking as soon as she appeared. Too abruptly or was she just being paranoid?

Hazel put the salad on the table, chatted for a few minutes before going out but she didn't go far. She waited just outside the door. It was stupid, she knew. Mum had been getting better, stronger, day on day until she was almost back to normal, back to her old self. So it couldn't be anything to do with that, could it? But Hazel hovered anyway, just to make sure. The doctors had warned that it could recur, of course: next week, next year, in twenty years or not at all. But Mum had promised to be open about it, promised to say if anything went wrong, if there was any hint of relapse.

Hazel waited. At first she heard nothing more than the clatter of dishes being arranged, re-arranged. It was OK. There was nothing wrong. She was just imagining things. Then just as she was about to move off Mum spoke.

'I thought it was all sorted,' she said wearily. 'Everything's been going so well.'

Hazel bit her lip to stop herself shouting out, pressed herself against the wall to stop herself bursting back into the room.

'It was,' said Sarah, 'more or less. And it will be. But you know what Christmas is like. I had to make it good for Lucy, didn't I? Her first Christmas! Aww go on, Mum. It's only a couple of hundred so I can pay off my credit card.'

Hazel stopped lip-biting, stopped pressing, stood up straight. Money! That's all it was. Nothing sinister. Just Sarah lapsing into her old ways. The final proof that life was getting back to some sort of normality!

'All right,' said Mum. 'But this is the last time, Sarah. Do you understand? And whatever you do, don't tell your dad!'

How, Dee wondered, as she huddled over her laptop trying to finish her work, had the holiday gone so fast? Three more days and they'd be back at school. Well at least they'd got through New Year's Day without a major crisis. OK so Dad had been more than usually quiet, Scott more than usually edgy but there'd been no direct reference to Lauren. To what had happened on New Year's Day two years ago. Gran had made sure of that by keeping them busy. Long walk in the morning that Kieran had whinged about, a late lunch with Gran's friends, which Kieran had said was boring, then, in the evening they'd split up, gone their separate ways to various parties.

God knows what Kieran's get-together with his mates had involved because he wouldn't say. He seemed to have spent half the holiday in bed but he'd sworn over and over that he wasn't into any sort of drugs. Stuck to his story that the money he'd nicked had all gone on cigarettes, drink, phone top-ups and arcade games. Not that any of that was much better! He'd still been pissing away other people's money, hadn't he? Behaving like a total prat. Not to mention breaking the law. But that was Kieran. And at least now Granddad was on his case, there was *some* hope.

Scott, of course, hadn't had anything planned for the evening and no way could they leave him home alone so she'd taken him with her to Hazel's family party where he'd spent most of the time out in the yard, happily playing with the dogs. Not even wincing when they jumped up at him. So that must mean he was getting better, mustn't it? Physically at least. It was hard to tell. He'd never take his top off, never let anyone see. Except the doctors, when Gran took him for his check-ups. But, even then, he wouldn't let Gran stay in the room while he was examined, like he was somehow embarrassed, ashamed, as though it was his fault not Lauren's.

The beep of a car horn interrupted her thoughts. She glanced at her watch. Sanjay! Sanjay was here already. By the time she'd shut down her laptop, grabbed her things and got downstairs, Scott had already let Sanjay in and was still hovering beside him in the narrow hall.

'You going into town?' Scott asked.

'Yeah,' Sanjay said. 'We're meeting Hazel and Joe to do some shopping. Oh joy!'

'Can I come?' said Scott. 'I won't hang around with you or anything. I want to buy some new games with my Christmas money.'

Dee could barely believe what she was hearing. Scott volunteering to go out, to go round town on his own? But should she let him? Would he be OK?

''Course,' said Sanjay before Dee could recover enough to answer. 'I might even come with you to look at games. Better than hanging round clothes shops,' he added, winking at Dee.

Was shopping for games really any better than clothes? Or had Sanjay just sensed her panic. It was stupid, she knew. Kieran was right when he had a go at her for being over-protective towards Scott. Scott would have been fine. But she was still glad when they arrived in town and Sanjay headed off with him.

Joe stuck with her and Hazel, patiently sitting outside changing rooms with a permanent, slightly vacant smile, like he couldn't really believe he'd finally managed to get it together with Hazel.

'Do you think I've done the right thing then?' Hazel asked, as she tried on yet another top. 'With Joe, I mean?'

'Yeah,' Dee said, 'why not? You've always seemed good together. Owww,' she added, struggling to zip up a pair of particularly tight jeans. 'I seriously need to diet. I've eaten tons over Christmas.'

'Oh, give up,' groaned Hazel. 'You're beginning to sound just like Abbie. *I had an orange for Christmas dinner. Can you believe that? A whole orange, all to myself. Tom says I'm such a pig!*'

Dee laughed. She could barely help it. Hazel had Abbie's over-the-top shriek to perfection but it wasn't really funny. Especially now when every mention of Abbie reminded her of their conversation; the story she should never have told her.

'No,' said Dee, as she finally squeezed herself into the jeans. 'No good! I need something I can actually move in.'

As she was taking them off her mobile rang.

'Get that, will you?' she asked Hazel. 'Right jacket pocket.'

'Hi, Sanjay. No, it's Hazel. Dee's standing around in her undies! What? It's a bit of a bad signal. Scott? Er, no. We haven't seen him, thought he was with you.'

Dee snatched the phone, trying to listen, trying to dress at the same time.

'OK. Right. I'll be there in a minute. Shit, shit, shit,' she mumbled, throwing on the rest of her clothes, shoving the phone back in her pocket, flinging open the changing room curtain.

'What's happened?' said Hazel, as they went out to where Joe was waiting.

'Not sure,' said Dee. 'Sanjay was looking at DVDs. He saw Scott over by the door talking to a kid from school. Jamie Smith, he thinks. Then the next minute Scott's running out. By the time Sanjay got outside Scott had disappeared.'

'Hang on,' said Hazel, grabbing Dee's arm as they got outside. 'Before you go chasing all over town, phone him, phone Scott.'

'Oh, right, yeah,' said Dee, pulling out her phone, pressing as she walked. 'I'm not thinking straight – he's not picking up. It's ringing but he's not answering. Hang on – Scott. Listen. Phone me, all right? Tell me where you are. Voice mail,' she added, for Hazel's benefit.

All the time Dee was tapping, talking, she was looking around, looking for Scott. She didn't see him but she saw Sanjay hurrying to meet them.

'Any sign?' Dee asked.

'No, but Jamie Smith thinks he went that way,' said Sanjay pointing up the high street. 'So maybe he's heading back to the car park or the bus station.'

'He probably won't know where he's going, what he's doing,' said Dee. 'What the hell happened? What did bloody Jamie Smith say to him?'

'Er, I talked to Jamie,' said Sanjay, 'after I phoned

135

you. He reckoned he hadn't said anything at first but I finally got summat out of him.'

'What?' Dee almost screamed.

'I didn't really get it,' said Sanjay. 'He's not over bright, is Jamie. Hard to know what he's on about, sometimes. Summat about scars. Said he only asked Scott if he could see his scars. I mean what scars? Has Scott got any scars?'

A sharp pain stabbed deep in Dee's stomach as if someone had kicked her. Yeah, Scott had scars. Dozens of them. But how did Jamie Smith know? No way would Scott have told him. Scott wouldn't have told anybody!

Apart from the family, apart from people back home who read the local paper at the time, there was only one other person who knew about the scars.

'Abbie!' she said, as she tried to keep walking, tried to keep pace with the others. 'Does Jamie Smith know Abbie?'

'Probably,' said Joe, rubbing his moustache, looking totally confused. 'He'll know who she is. I mean everyone knows everyone round here, don't they? Why?'

'Yeah but are they neighbours or anything?' Dee persisted. 'Are their families friends or anything?'

Hazel was shaking her head.

'What about brothers and sisters, then?' said Dee. 'Has Jamie got older brothers, sisters?'

'Dozens,' said Hazel, 'if you count all the halves and steps. Complicated set-up. Why? And what's it got to do with Abbie?'

'Well is she mates with any of them?'

'Don't think so,' said Hazel. 'I mean, one of them – Cherry or Kerry, I think she's called – works up at Tom's hotel. But she's hardly a mate. Abbie can't stand her. Reckons she's a right tart who keeps coming onto Tom.'

'Probably the other way round,' Sanjay muttered.

'It doesn't matter what bloody way round it is,' Dee snapped. 'She's told someone. Abbie's told someone, up at the hotel. She must have done! This Kerry-Cherry person's picked up on it...spread it around.'

'Spread what around?' said Joe. 'I don't get it.'

'Neither do I,' said Hazel, glancing at Dee. 'But the main thing we need to do is find Scott, right? So we ought to split up. Let Sanjay try the bus station. Joe can do the car park. And we'll give Scott's mobile another go. Maybe ring your grandparents as well, eh?'

'No, not yet,' said Dee, as the lads went off. 'It's only been ten minutes. He can't have got far. He must still be in town somewhere. I'll try his mobile again, like you said.'

She stood, leaning against the wall of the bank, listening to Scott's phone ring out.

'Look,' said Hazel. 'I don't want to make this any worse or pry or anything but just how bad is this? I

137

mean Scott's not like gonna do anything stupid, is he?'

'No,' said Dee. 'I don't think so. Not like you mean. But something like this could really flip him out, could set him back months. And it's all my fault. Why was I so bloody stupid! Why did I tell her?'

'This is Abbie, right? That day at the end of term, I guess? You weren't just talking about Sanjay, like you said? You told her something about Scott?'

'Yeah, that and a whole load of other stuff.'

Dee pulled herself away from the wall as a phone rang. But it wasn't her phone. Wrong tone. Besides, she still had her phone clutched to her ear, listening to Scott's answering service over and over. Hazel's phone, then.

'Great!' Hazel was already saying. 'Oh. No. Right. Well, don't do anything! We'll be there in a minute.'

Hazel shoved the phone back in her pocket and grabbed Dee's arm.

'Come on,' she said. 'It's Joe. He's found Scott.'

They met up with Joe in the car park. He was looking towards a patch of wasteland at the back, still full of debris where a couple of old shops had been demolished to make way for a car park extension. At first Dee didn't see anything except rubble then she caught a hint, a blur of movement. Scott was sitting on the ground, in a slight hollow; hunched, head down, hands clasped round his knees, gently rocking. His new jacket, the one Gran had bought him for Christmas, was lying in the mud with his discarded jumper and T-shirt.

'I phoned Sanjay too,' Joe said. 'He's on his way. But I didn't know what to do about...'

He was talking to himself. The girls were already moving towards Scott.

'Slowly,' Dee warned Hazel, as they approached.

She could see Scott was shivering as well as rocking. No wonder, in this weather with his back, his arms all exposed. Why had he done that? Taken his tops off? It was weird – the very last thing she'd expect him to do. But who could tell what was going on in his head? She picked up his jacket, draped it round him, while Hazel picked up the jumper and T-shirt.

'It's OK,' Dee said. 'It's OK.'

'He knows,' Scott murmured, still hunched, huddled. 'He'll tell everybody. He knows.'

Dee tried to fasten the jacket round him as she helped him up, knotting the sleeves at the front almost like a bloody straitjacket, but she wasn't quite quick enough. Hazel's sharp intake of breath told Dee that she'd seen. You could hardly fail to see the scars on his arms. But there were more. And it was worse; worse even than Dee had imagined.

She led Scott, his whole body tense, rigid, over to Sanjay's car. The lads were already there, trying not to look at the small areas of Scott's chest and stomach that were still exposed, trying not to see the criss-cross of tightly puckered, mutilated skin, the unnatural whiteness of the slow-healing wounds.

Sitting with Scott in the back of the car, Dee was aware of Hazel saying something before Sanjay closed the door, was aware of Hazel and Joe standing, watching them, curious and confused as they drove off. Sanjay said nothing, nothing at all. What was there to say? She'd have to tell them, of course. Sometime. Sometime soon. She couldn't just let them piece it together from the patchy, exaggerated rumours that would filter round. Exaggerated? How could you exaggerate something like that? How could you make it any worse than it was? Her arm automatically tightened around Scott who was sobbing now. The deep, gasping sounds from his throat telling her he was re-living it yet again. Coming home early that New Year's Day, two years ago...

They'd all been despatched somewhere on New Year's Eve so Lauren and Dad could have their quality time, their romantic meal together at some posh restaurant. Kieran hadn't needed despatching. He was already in Italy, skiing with his mate Billy's family. Lauren had reluctantly allowed Dee to go to

Nana and Pops. But Scott – Scott was just five doors down the road, staying with one of his school friends. Only his friend had been ill in the night. Too much party food, too much excitement maybe. Puking all over the place.

'The bedroom stank,' Scott would tell them later, much later. 'An' he was still throwing up in the morning so I decided to go home.'

But what Scott didn't know, what he couldn't possibly know, was that Dad and Lauren hadn't ever been to bed; that their night had been a total disaster. Bumping into old friends of Dad's in the restaurant. Three couples. One of the women noticeably pregnant. Agreeing to go back to the pregnant woman's house for drinks. Lauren fine, if drinking heavily.

'Not driving, am I?' she'd said. 'And I'm certainly not pregnant. So no worries there, eh, Peter?'

Warnings. Especially when Lauren realised one of the other ladies wasn't drinking either.

'You driving, then?' she'd asked.

Then it had come, the simpered response. Dee hadn't heard it, of course, not at first hand, but she could imagine the scene in every detail.

'Well, no actually. I'm expecting too. Only two months. Haven't told many people yet. In fact, you're the first – outside the family.'

Lauren hadn't kicked off then. It wasn't Lauren's way. She'd poured herself another drink, offered congratulations.

'Isn't that wonderful? Two happy events! Or are you pregnant too?' she'd asked the third lady.

'Hope not,' the lady had said, sipping wine. 'The twins are only ten months, couldn't cope with another just yet. You two don't know what you're letting yourself in for!' she'd joked, launching a whole night of baby talk.

Every word lodging in Lauren's mind to be spewed out later in a storm of abuse and blows when they got home in the early hours. A storm that was still raging when Scott got home. He'd known something was wrong because the front door was open. Not just unlocked but actually open. At first, seeing a hall table overturned, he'd feared a burglary until he'd heard the yell from the kitchen.

'No it's not bloody all right, Peter,' Lauren had screamed. 'That fat, sanctimonious cow waddling around showing off her bulge, like she's the only woman in the world to have a sodding baby! But she isn't, is she? They can all have them, can't they? And you know why, Peter? Because they're married to real men, not useless bloody wimps like you.'

Maybe those weren't the exact words. It had all been patched together from what Scott and Dad had told the police later. There was probably more swearing. More verbal abuse that had somehow got lost, swallowed up by what happened next. And Scott had stood there, listening, frozen in the hallway, not knowing what to do. He was barely nine. How could he have known? Known how bad it was going to get.

A sudden violent shiver from Scott brought Dee back to the present. Was he there too, in that hallway? Had he reached the same point in the memories? Or was he somewhere else? Further on? Further back? And, wherever he was, should she try to bring him out of it? But how could she? She couldn't even stop herself. Already Lauren's next words were shrieking in Dee's head.

'You planned it, didn't you, Peter?'

That crazy, crazy accusation, repeated over and over!

'You planned it! Just to hurt me. You knew they'd be there, at the restaurant with all their wonderful news, didn't you? Well, come on then,' she'd yelled, grabbing a bottle of champagne that had been left over from Christmas. 'Let's celebrate. Let's toast your smarmy friends and all their lovely little babies and happy bloody families.'

'Lauren, no,' Dad had said.

She was holding the bottle by the neck, waving it around shouting, swearing, not knowing that someone else was watching; that Scott had moved slowly, silently to the kitchen doorway. Dad leant forward to try and grab the bottle but a brief glimpse of Scott momentarily distracted him and, in that instant, it happened.

Did she mean to do it? Did Lauren mean to hit Dad? Or was she just swinging the champagne bottle round, wildly, randomly? Either way the heavy base cracked against Dad's forehead. The bottle didn't even break. Not then. But the force had been enough to knock Dad out, to send him crashing into a chair, slumping to the floor, dragging the chair on top of him.

That's when Scott first cried out. When he saw Dad lying there, not moving, bubbles of blood oozing from a single deep cut above his right eye. Scott's cry made Lauren swing round, dropping the bottle, which smashed on the tiled floor, fizzing champagne everywhere, making Scott slip, twist his ankle, as he pushed past Lauren to get to Dad.

'He still wasn't moving,' Scott had screamed during one of his interviews with the police. 'She said it was an accident. She kept saying it was an accident. Kept saying that she loved him. But he wasn't moving. I thought he was dead!'

Scott had scrambled up, feeling for a phone in his trouser pocket. But he didn't manage to get it out because Lauren had picked something up. The broken bottle. The biggest, sharpest piece. Stood blocking Scott's way, eyes glazed but blazing at the same time, was how Scott described it.

'Like there was no one really there inside her head, like she wasn't even human any more.'

Slashing out with the razor-sharp glass, slicing through Scott's sweatshirt, jabbing into his stomach, his chest. And all the time Dad was lying there, unconscious, unable to help.

'You're not going to tell,' Lauren had screamed, aiming higher so that Scott had to put his arms up to protect his neck, his face. 'I won't let you spoil everything. I love him. I didn't mean it. I love him.'

'It didn't hurt,' Scott had once told a therapist. 'Not then. I didn't feel anything. I didn't know I was bleeding or nothing.'

Shock. He was already half in shock, which is probably what saved him. Because if he'd known how many gashes there were, how deep some of them went, if he'd seen the blood, been aware of it soaking through what was left of his clothes, dripping onto the floor, he'd never have been able to do what he did. In fact, Dee still wasn't sure how Scott had eventually managed to get past Lauren, lock himself in the bathroom. But he had. He'd phoned the emergency services too but by the time they got there, he'd passed out and they'd had to break the door down to get to him. Lauren had gone by then, of course. The police had picked her up two days later at Heathrow.

'Hey.'

Someone was speaking to her. Not then but here, now, in the present. Sanjay. He was opening the car door.

'Do you want me to stay?' he said. 'Help get him inside?'

She nodded, swallowed, pushing back tears. There wasn't time to cry. She had to get Scott sorted. Tell Gran and Granddad what had happened. Then there was Dad. How the hell was she going to handle all that?

11

It was freezing, literally. Hazel rubbed her foot across an icy puddle as she stood outside Mrs Mitchell's unit on Monday lunchtime, waiting for Dee to come out. It was the third week of term and Scott had only just come back. Hardly any wonder, after what had happened. The state he'd got into.

Hazel dug her heel into the ice, cracking it, watching it splinter. It was almost unbelievable, what Dee had finally told them – about Lauren. Like something out of a horror film. Something that didn't happen, shouldn't happen in real life, to real people. But it did. More often than you'd think, Dee had said.

'How's it going?' Hazel asked, when Dee appeared.

'He's managing,' Dee said. 'Mrs Mitchell's great, isn't she? He'll probably stay in the unit all week then start filtering back into lessons slowly again. It's a mess but...'

'What?'

'I dunno,' said Dee. 'It's not been as bad as I thought, I suppose. It all coming out and everything. I mean, everyone's been really good – teachers, friends. And at home too. Did I tell you Dad took Scott to see his own therapist?'

Hazel shook her head as they started to wander across the playground.

'Yeah, she doesn't usually work with children. Don't know why. But she's been brill for Dad so he talked her into seeing Scott too. I mean, that was good in itself. That Dad was even motivated enough to ask.'

'And it's helped?' Hazel asked.

'I think so,' said Dee. 'It's helped Dad more than it's helped Scott. But then he's been seeing her longer. It's all very slow but I think it's down to the therapist that Scott's back in school. So, yeah, we're getting there.'

Did Dee really mean all that or was she just trying to be positive? They still hadn't found out exactly how the story had got round but, by the time they'd got back to school after New Year, it was obvious that a fair few people knew. Hazel had wanted to phone Abbie, ask her outright whether it had started with her but Dee had said no.

'It might not have been Abbie,' Dee had said. 'Anyone could have come across the story, couldn't they, on the net or something?'

148

Yeah, right! So Hazel had ignored Dee, gone behind her back, tried to phone Abbie a couple of times but the number was unobtainable and when she'd tried the hotel, she'd been told that Abbie wasn't there or was busy. She'd left messages but, of course, Abbie hadn't bothered phoning back. Even if she had, she'd probably have denied everything, wouldn't she?

'Hey, what's going on over there?' said Joe, suddenly coming up to join them. 'Looks like a fight or something.'

Hazel followed the direction of his gaze to where a small crowd had gathered. But it didn't look or sound like the sort of noisy crowd that hovered round a fight. It was mainly girls for a start, older girls at that. A few lads. Sanjay was there, on the fringe, looking at his feet rather than at what was going on.

'Oh, wow!' Hazel heard one girl shout out, as they got closer.

'Are those stones for *real*?' someone asked.

Then another voice, an unmistakable voice, rising above the rest.

''Course they're real. Sapphire and diamond. Tom says he'll just kill me if I lose it or anything!'

Hazel pushed her way forward until she could see Abbie standing in the centre, left hand extended, flashing the ring that must have cost a fortune. Like the

149

coat Abbie was wearing and the boots. Instinctively Hazel turned to leave, to get Dee out of the way, but Abbie had already seen them.

'Hey,' she called out, breaking free of her circle of fans. 'Hazel, Dee. Wait up.'

Before Hazel could escape, Abbie was there, barging between her and Dee, leaving Joe somewhere to the side, excluded until he got the hint and went to join Sanjay. This was obviously going to be girl talk.

'I've been looking for you!' Abbie announced, smiling first at Hazel, then at Dee. 'I've been wanting to pop in for ages but we've been so busy up at the hotel, I haven't had a minute. So, what do you think?' she asked, waving her hand around again.

'You're engaged, right?' Hazel said.

'Totally, totally right!' said Abbie.

'Didn't think anybody bothered with stuff like that anymore,' said Hazel.

'Tom's not just anybody,' said Abbie. 'And you could at least be pleased for me.'

But she said it smiling, casual, like she didn't much care whether they were pleased or not.

'I mean, we didn't really plan it or anything,' Abbie went on. 'But we just happened to look in this jeweller's when we were Christmas shopping and I like saw this ring but I'm like trying not to look 'cos I don't want Tom to think I'm dropping hints or anything but he

150

must have noticed, see? So then...on Christmas morning – get this – this is like just so romantic...'

On and on she went, describing every detail, every word that Tom said; not noticing that her reception was icier than the weather.

'Tom wants us to get married this summer but his parents reckon we should wait a while with me being a bit young and us not having been together long and all that. But like Tom says, why wait when you're sure? Still, he's got to be a bit careful 'cos they've got all the money! But...'

She giggled, looked down at her ring again.

'There's something else I wanna tell you,' Abbie said, as if suddenly aware she didn't really have their attention. 'But it's a secret, right?'

'So what do *your* mum and dad think?' Hazel asked, before Abbie could start on another wildly exaggerated Tom story, secret or otherwise. 'About getting engaged?'

'Don't think they know,' said Abbie, more quietly. 'Went round to take their presents on Christmas Eve, had another massive row and that was it, really. Haven't seen or heard from them since. Well, Mum kept leaving messages on my phone for a while but Tom said not to answer them 'cos I'd only get all upset again if I spoke to her. An' he was right 'cos even the messages were sort of freaking me, so after New Year Tom got my number changed and he's told reception not to put anyone through to me, if they call the hotel.'

'Abbie, don't you think . . . ' Hazel began.

She stopped herself. There was no point. No point trying to suggest she make up with her parents. Abbie wouldn't listen. She was already off again on one of her monologues.

'Anyway, how's things with you two? School as boring as ever? Bit quieter without me around, eh? Hey, I heard summat about you the other day, Hazel. Someone said you'd got together with Joe. Can you believe the stuff that gets round? You and Joe! I mean, I said to Tom – no way! Hazel can do *way* better for herself than that.'

'So what's wrong with Joe?' Dee asked, speaking for the first time.

'Nothing apart from being dead scruffy, pig-headed and pig-ugly.'

Abbie paused, staring at Hazel, before giving a little, forced laugh.

'Whoops. I've put my foot in it, haven't I? I mean, he's not really that gross or anything. We've never exactly got on 'cos he's never really liked me, has he? But I suppose he's sort of nice, in his own way, and . . . '

'It doesn't matter,' Hazel snapped. 'We can't all be lucky enough to have a Tom, can we? But talking of stuff getting round . . . did you blab about—'

She caught Dee's glance, tried to stop but it was too late; the rest of the question came gushing out.

'No!' said Abbie. 'What do you take me for? I wouldn't spread nothing like that around. Honest I wouldn't.'

'So you didn't tell anyone?' Hazel said.

'No,' Abbie repeated. '"Cept Tom, of course, 'cos me'an' Tom tell each other everything. But half the time he doesn't listen – 'specially to anything about school or my friends and stuff. So *he* won't have said anything, will he? Why?'

'I think he might,' said Hazel. 'I think he might have told Cherry Smith.'

'Kerry,' said Abbie, her cheeks suddenly reddening at the same time as Dee's turned pale. 'It's Kerry. Kerry Smith.'

'That'd be Kerry whose step-brother's in Scott's class?' said Hazel. 'The one who asked Scott whether he could see his scars. The one who'd told half the class why Scott doesn't do PE before the teachers could shut him up.'

'Oh,' said Abbie.

'Is that it?' said Hazel. 'Is that all you're going to say? I mean, you wouldn't like to apologise to Dee or ask about Scott or anything?'

'Yeah, I'm sorry,' said Abbie. 'But it wasn't my fault if Tom blabbed, was it? I mean, why would he tell Kerry of all people? Sure he laughs and jokes with her

153

but he does that with all the girls . . . Paige, everyone. It's part of his job, he says, to be nice to the staff. He doesn't even like bloody Kerry, or so he says!'

'Is that all you care about?' said Hazel. 'How cosy Tom is with Kerry? You don't give a toss about Dee or Scott, do you?'

'Leave it, Hazel,' said Dee. 'It doesn't matter, now.'

'It does matter, though,' said Hazel, looking at Dee, then back at Abbie. 'I don't believe this. I really don't know you anymore, Abbie. And you know what? I don't think I want to either.'

Abbie looked, for a moment, as if she was going to cry.

'Fine,' she said before turning, walking off. 'That's just fine by me.'

Abbie hurried down the drive without looking back. It wasn't fair. Why did everyone have to spoil things all the time? This was the first bit of freedom, the first day off work, she'd had for ages.

'Why don't you go into school?' Tom had suggested. 'See your old mates, while I get all this paperwork done? I'll book you a taxi, eh?'

Bloody great! So now she'd have to get a taxi back 'cos she couldn't disturb Tom when he was doing the rotas and stuff. She stopped at the bottom of the school drive, phoned a taxi and walked on to the square where she'd arranged to meet it. Well away from the school, well away from bloody Hazel whingeing on about Scott.

She shuddered, rubbing her arms while she waited. It might have been Tom who'd blabbed. She hadn't been quite straight with Hazel about that. How could she have been? How could she have told her about Tom's reaction, with Dee standing right there? *Half the time he doesn't listen*. That bit had been true. Tom didn't listen – usually. But he'd listened to that particular story.

'Hang on,' he'd said. 'So this Dee person thought I was knocking you about? Then she tells you this sob-story about her wicked stepmother? Load of balls, then, isn't it?'

'No! It's true,' she'd insisted. 'You weren't there. You didn't see how upset Dee was.'

Tom had been high on something. He must have been 'cos he'd started laughing.

'God, Abbie, you're just so naive. Fall for anything, you would. OK so "wicked stepmum" might have slapped Scott around a bit but slicing him up – no way! It's just daft, innit? Not to mention a complete waste of champagne!'

Is that how he'd told it to Kerry? As some sort of joke! While they were standing at the bar, arms wrapped round each other, like they did. Not that the cuddling and stuff meant anything. Tom told her that all the time. That's sort of why they'd got engaged. Something else she hadn't been quite straight with Hazel about. Sure it had been dead romantic, in a way. The tiny box nestled in the bunch of red roses. But then Tom had spoilt it later when she'd been showing Paige and Leo.

'Thought it'd stop Abbie whingeing,' Tom had said. 'If I proved I was serious. And I am,' he'd added, putting his arms round her. 'Abbie's the only girl for me.'

But he'd said it in a way that had set Paige and Leo off laughing. It had set Paige off on something else too – watching Abbie all the time, hovering around her during breaks, looking at her when they were working until Abbie had finally got fed up with it.

'Summat wrong?' she'd asked.

'No, not really,' Paige had said, all sickly, smarmy. 'Look – don't take this the wrong way – 'cos I'm only trying to help – but do you really know what you're doing with Tom?'

'Meaning?'

'Meaning Tom's all right, he's a good laugh and all that. But he's never gonna settle down, you know. Not in the way you want. He's a classic avoidant. And you just don't see it, do you?'

See it? She hadn't had the foggiest clue what Paige was on about. She wasn't going to show her ignorance, wasn't going to ask, but Paige must have seen her confusion 'cos she explained anyway.

'An avoidant,' she said, as if she was spouting from a psychology text book, 'can't commit. Tries. Goes through the motions. Might even marry. But they're terrified of getting really close. I know,' she'd added, giggling almost nervously. 'Trust me. I'm a bit that way myself. That's why I hang around with Leo 'cos he doesn't want long-term serious neither.'

'Yeah, well, what you and Leo do is your business but leave me and Tom out of it.'

'I tried,' Paige had said, shrugging. 'Didn't expect you to listen but I tried. You're way out of your league, sweetie.'

Sweetie! She hated the way Paige talked down to her like that. And why, why had Paige told her all that rubbish at all? 'Cos she was jealous, 'cos her own relationship with Leo wasn't going anywhere? 'Cos she was a crap actress who never got any roles? 'Cos she fancied Tom herself? It sure as hell wasn't the reason she gave:

'I like you, Abbie. Believe it or not, I've actually started to like you. And I just feel so sorry for you.'

She didn't want Paige to feel sorry for her. She didn't need anyone's sympathy. Especially not now. Now she had her little secret. She'd nearly blurted it out to Hazel but she was glad she hadn't. Tom. Tom was the one to tell first. Even though she wasn't a hundred per cent sure.

The taxi beeped as it drew up. Abbie clambered in. She'd go home, back to the hotel. Tell him now. Why not? He'd be pleased, wouldn't he? He'd said as much a while back when she'd stupidly forgotten to re-order her pills.

'Quit panicking,' he'd said. 'It'll be all right. And if anything happens, so what? It'd be great, wouldn't it? Having a Tom junior around.'

Which sort of proved that what Paige had said was wrong, didn't it? Tom wasn't avoiding commitment. No way. He was gonna be sooo pleased when she told him.

12

Tom wasn't in his office when Abbie got back and she wasn't the only person looking for him.

'Where is he?' Tom's father asked, storming out of his office opposite. 'Have you seen him?'

Abbie shook her head. She could rarely summon the courage to talk to either of Tom's parents. Not that they ever stayed still long enough for any real conversation. They were always on the go. Total stress-heads, workaholics Tom said when he talked about them at all, which wasn't very often.

'I've just got back from my meeting,' Tom's dad was ranting, 'thinking all the rotas would be done but he hasn't even touched them! He's not answering his phone so I expect I'll end up doing them myself, as usual. Try his room, will you?' he added, thrusting his hand into his pocket, handing her a bunch of keys. 'Tell him I want him down here. Now!'

Tom's room wasn't with the rest of the staff quarters;

it was at the top of what his mother grandly called the 'East Wing'. And it wasn't just a room either. It was a whole apartment. It was brill up there, totally isolated. Even the lift didn't go that far. You had to get off at the fourth floor and use the stairs, hidden behind a door marked 'private'. It was locked so she used the key from the bunch Tom's dad had given her. She was supposed to be getting her own soon, when Tom got round to having one cut.

The top of the stairs opened direct into Tom's hallway and, as soon as Abbie got up there, she heard a voice, a female voice, coming from along the corridor. Paige. She was sure it was Paige. OK, no big deal. Paige and one or two of the others often came up to work out in Tom's gym. But the voice wasn't coming from the small gym or his sitting room; it was coming from the bedroom.

Abbie paused outside, certain that whoever was in there would be able to hear her heart thudding. Tom. Tom was in there too. She could hear him laughing. Tom. Tom and Paige. In his bedroom. Together. She edged back. She didn't want to see, didn't want to know. Or did she? She hovered, uncertainly. It had gone quiet. Should she knock? Cough? Creep away? Oh God, it couldn't be. It couldn't be what she thought. Tom wouldn't do that to her. He wouldn't. They were just talking, maybe.

She almost clapped, jumped up and down when she heard them. The other voices. Leo. Surely that was Leo? And Kerry. Tom and Paige weren't alone. It was one of Tom's little parties. The sort she didn't like. The sort Tom knew she didn't like. That's why he'd been so keen for her to go into school to see her mates. Leo had been away over the weekend. Probably come back with some stuff. Not brilliant, especially after Tom's New Year's resolution to stop, but at least it wasn't what she thought.

She moved towards the door again, knocked, pushed it open and stared, unable to believe what she was seeing.

'O-my-god, Abbie!' she heard Tom say above the sound of her own shriek.

A shriek that went on and on as she dropped the keys, ran back along the narrow corridor, down the stairs, out onto the fourth floor, not bothering to wait for the lift. More stairs, out past reception, almost knocking over a couple of guests in her hurry to get outside. Still crying, running, slipping on the icy drive, banging her knee, hardly feeling, hardly caring as she got up, carried on running – where?

She stopped, got out her phone, her fingers barely able to press the buttons. Who was she calling anyway? She didn't know. Scrolling down her numbers; all the time battling to get the images out of her head. The images of that room. What she'd seen. But she couldn't. The phone was trembling in her shaking hand, the driveway was spinning making her feel sick, dizzy until she couldn't even stand any more. She flopped down onto the cold, grassy verge.

'*You're way out of your league, sweetie.*'

Was that it? Was that what Paige was trying to warn her about? Something she would never have believed – could barely have imagined.

'Hello? Abbie?'

Faint voice, coming from her phone. She'd called someone. By mistake. It didn't matter. Somebody, anybody, would do.

'Come and get me,' she yelled into the phone. 'Please. Get me away from here.'

Dee and Scott were almost back home when a car drew up beside them. Dee turned to see Sanjay, leaning over, opening the passenger door. What the heck was *he* doing here? He was supposed to be back at school, practising with his band.

'Will Scott be all right on his own?' Sanjay asked looking towards Gran's house.

'Yeah,' said Dee. 'I'll just see him in. Gran'll be there. Why? What's wrong?'

'Hurry up,' was all Sanjay said.

Dee almost shoved Scott into the house, dropped her bag in the hall and hurried back to the car. She'd barely closed the door when Sanjay set off.

'Sanjay,' she said, struggling to fasten her seat belt. 'What the hell is going on? And slow down!'

'Yeah, sorry,' he said, slowing to the speed limit. 'It's Abbie. She phoned me. She's in a real state.'

'What sort of state?' said Dee. 'She was fine a couple of hours ago. Had a bit of a row with Hazel but that wouldn't bother her overmuch, would it?'

'I don't know. Couldn't make out most of what she said. She wants me to pick her up from the hotel. Sounded totally hysterical so I thought it might be best if I took you with me.'

'Gee thanks! That's just what I need. Another dose of Abbie today.'

'Sorry,' said Sanjay again. 'Probably turn out to be nothing much. You know what she's like.'

Dee knew exactly what Abbie was like but she was still unprepared for what they saw as they swung into the hotel drive. Abbie was standing on the grass verge, her face a mass of black streaks and red blotches, her cream-coloured coat filthy, her arms waving – keeping Tom away. Tom shivered in a T-shirt, jeans, belt hanging open. Shoes but no socks, like he'd dressed in a hurry.

'Don't touch me!' Dee heard Abbie yell as they got out of the car. 'Don't come near me.'

'It didn't mean anything,' Tom was saying at the same time. 'Oh come on! Don't be such a kid, Abbie. What I

163

was doing – it's nothing to do with you and me. It's just a bit of fun.'

'Fun!' Abbie screamed.

'Look, I'm sorry, OK. It won't happen again. Not ever. Abbie! Don't be stupid. You don't have to go.'

He was talking to himself. Abbie had already climbed into the back of Sanjay's car, was sitting hunched in the corner, her head down.

'What have you done, you bastard?' Sanjay was asking, moving towards Tom until Dee pulled him away.

'Just drive,' said Dee, scrambling into the back, next to Abbie. 'Let's get her home.'

'No,' said Abbie, quietly. 'Not home. I can't go home.'

'Yes you can,' said Dee. 'Whatever's happened, your mum'll help. She'll know…'

'She can't,' said Abbie, her voice tight, controlled, like she was trying to stop herself screaming. 'She can't help. Nobody can. I'm pregnant. I think I'm pregnant.'

'Pregnant?' said Dee, trying to piece this information together with what she'd heard, what she'd seen, knowing it didn't quite fit. 'And Tom's said he doesn't want it, or something?'

'*I* don't want it,' said Abbie starting to cry. 'Tom doesn't know. I didn't tell him. Because he was in there with Kerry and Paige and Leo and they were – I don't want it. I don't want his baby. I don't want him. How could he do that? How could he?'

All attempt at control gone, Abbie's voice had risen to a screech as she wound down the window, pulled off her ring and hurled it out onto the road. She kept the window open, her head half hanging out as freezing air blasted through the car.

'Hey,' said Dee, trying to draw her back.

But it was no good. Abbie's limbs had gone rigid, like a toddler in a tantrum. She was groaning, crying, repeating things over and over. About what Tom had been doing.

'Watch the road,' Dee told Sanjay as his glances in the rear-view mirror became more frequent.

At first Dee hadn't really understood what Abbie was on about. And now – now it was all becoming clearer – it was making her feel ill. So what the hell must it have been like for Abbie? Walking in on something like that? A scene straight out of some sleazy porn mag. Starring your own boyfriend, the father of your baby.

'He said everyone does stuff like that, these days,' Abbie was saying for about the eighth time. 'But they don't, do they?'

'No,' said Dee. 'No, they don't. It's Tom's choice, I guess, but it doesn't have to be yours.'

The car had come to a stop outside a house. Modern, detached. Abbie's, presumably. Dee had never been to Abbie's before. Sanjay had got out, opened the car door for Abbie but she didn't move. She just sat there shaking her head so eventually Dee got out, walked up to the house and rang the bell.

Abbie's mum appeared.

'Er, I'm a friend of Abbie's,' Dee began, looking back towards the car.

'Something's happened?' Abbie's mum said, her whole face creasing, crumbling as she spoke. 'She's had an accident?'

'No, not an accident,' Dee said hastily. 'She's OK. She's not ill.'

By the time they'd walked down the path, Sanjay had managed to get Abbie out of the car. Her mum hurried towards her, hugged her, held her, talked to her while Dee stood listening, watching, transfixed almost. Whatever Abbie had said to her mum over the past few months, whatever she'd done, however much she'd hurt her, it was all gone, forgotten. Every word, every gesture from Abbie's mum oozed total, unconditional love; so much that Dee almost envied Abbie as her mum began to steer her towards the house.

'Thank you,' Abbie's mum said, suddenly turning back towards them. 'Thanks for bringing her home.'

Dee knew they were being dismissed. Not in a nasty way but definitely dismissed. She glanced at Sanjay who was having even more difficulty pulling himself away. But, unlike Dee, it wasn't Abbie's mum he was looking at, it was Abbie.

'Do we say anything?' Sanjay asked, on their mainly silent drive home. 'To Hazel or Joe or anyone?'

'Yeah,' said Dee, 'but only those two. And only the basics, eh? Just that she's split with Tom. Leave it to Abbie. It's up to her if she wants to tell anyone the details.'

Abbie did, it seemed. On Friday morning Hazel was waiting for Dee, pulling her into an empty classroom almost the minute she walked into school.

'I went round to Abbie's last night,' Hazel said. 'I wasn't going to,' she went on before Dee could respond. 'Mum said I shouldn't get involved but Abbie's been texting me all week, saying she needed to see me so I went and ... I know this sounds awful but now I wish I hadn't.'

'Why?' said Dee, though she had a fair idea.

'What she told me, about Tom, what he was doing – and she was crying all the time. So in the end she sets me off as well. Then last night I just couldn't sleep for thinking about it all.'

Dee nodded. She'd lost a fair amount of sleep herself recently.

'Crazy thing is,' said Hazel, 'I don't even think Abbie was that surprised. About what Tom did. Not deep down. I got the feeling she'd known for a while that there was stuff going on. Just didn't want to see it, didn't want to think about it.'

'Because when things were going well,' said Dee, almost automatically, 'they were really, really great, weren't they? Like with Dad and Lauren. That's what keeps you hooked. And I bet, in his own little way, Tom even meant most of the things he said.'

'You could be right,' said Hazel. 'He's still trying to get in touch with her but Abbie won't talk to him or anything.'

'So he still doesn't know about the baby?'

'Don't think so,' said Hazel, looking around, making sure no one was walking past, lurking in the doorway. 'Her mum's made her an appointment. At a clinic. Just for a sort of preliminary chat – you know? Talk through the options.'

'Are there any?' said Dee. 'I mean, she seemed pretty sure . . . '

'She keeps changing her mind,' said Hazel, 'almost by the minute. Can't bear to go ahead with it but can't face the idea of a termination either. Her parents say they'll support her whatever she decides so she kept asking me what I thought, what I'd do if I was her. But how can you answer summat like that? I mean nobody likes the thought of abortion, do they? But what if she has the baby and then she can't cope?'

'If her mum's helping . . . '

'I didn't mean the practical sort of things,' said Hazel. 'I meant with like Tom and stuff. What if he wants access? That's what worries Abbie most, I think, being forced into some sort of contact with him.'

'So what about adoption?' Dee asked. 'Has she thought about that?'

'Yeah but she reckons that would be worse than anything; having the baby, giving it up, knowing it was growing up somewhere, thinking about it all the time.'

Dee shook her head as the bell went. Hazel was right. There were no answers. No solutions. Not easy ones anyway.

'There was something else,' Hazel said, as they walked down the corridor. 'I'm not sure I should really say anything but . . .'

'Sanjay,' said Dee. 'He was round at Abbie's, right?'

'He turned up just as I was leaving, yeah. But he obviously told you, so that's OK.'

Dee nodded. Sanjay had been totally open about it. He'd known Abbie for years. He couldn't let her down now, could he? Nothing was going to happen, he'd stressed. And he was probably right. Even so . . .

'I've told Sanjay it might be best if we split,' said Dee, 'at least for a while.'

'Oh,' said Hazel, the one short word prompting Dee to go on, to explain.

'Guess I just can't cope with being second best,' said Dee, smiling, trying to keep it light.

'You're not!' said Hazel. 'Sanjay's been happier with you than he ever was with Abbie mucking him about all the time. And he's a total idiot if he lets you go. I mean, if anyone's second best it's Sanjay for Abbie. Sometime down the line there's gonna be another Tom, isn't there? And it's going to take her a fair while to get over this one – however much she says she hates him now.'

Did Abbie hate Tom? Probably not. Dee had a feeling that despite everything part of Abbie still loved him. If she had any sense, she wouldn't ever go back to him but that wouldn't stop her loving him. Just like there was a tiny, tiny part of Dad, hidden away somewhere, that still loved Lauren. And a bigger part that hated himself for ever loving her at all. Confusion. Mixed-up, tangled emotions – that's what made it so very hard to move on. In the end though, you had to. Maybe not quite in the direction you planned or the way that you wanted but, somehow, you had to keep going.

Dee stumbled slightly as some junior lads pushed past her. This time next year, with any luck, that could be Scott, hurrying to games, football boots tied to his bag. Dad might have a job. They could even have moved into their own house. Kieran might have matured, wised-up a bit so Gran and Granddad would finally be free to go on their cruise. OK, so she might be in flying pigs territory with Kieran but the rest was possible, wasn't it?

She, Hazel and Joe would probably be panicking about exams, trying to plan their futures. University, college, work? All going their separate ways or keeping in touch? Keeping in touch, she hoped, but who could tell?

Sanjay wouldn't be around. He'd be at Uni, surely? So if she didn't lose him to Abbie, would she lose him to some other girl in Sheffield, Leeds or wherever? Or was it like Sanjay had said when she suggested the split? That he still wanted to be with her; that it was her own insecurity driving them apart? Was there still a chance for them?

'You've gone all quiet,' Hazel said, holding the form room door open for her. 'What you thinking about?'

'Nothing,' said Dee, 'nothing much.'

It seemed stupid to say she was trying to look into the future. Because no one could do that, could they? So maybe it was best just to concentrate on the next five minutes. 'One step at a time,' as Dad's latest therapist was so fond of saying. Even so, as Dee sat down she couldn't help wondering about Abbie. What would Abbie be doing this time next year? What decision would she make?

Dee didn't know, couldn't be sure, didn't really know her well enough but Abbie was a survivor. However bad she felt now, whatever choices she made, she'd bounce back. Sooner or later, Abbie would get through it, be back to her old self, or something pretty close.

In fact, staring out of the window Dee could almost see her, hear her – Abbie standing out in that playground, surrounded by her usual crowd of fans. Telling them about a new job or college course she'd just started. And maybe – just maybe – showing off her baby.